THE DRAUGHTSMAN
AND THE UNICORN

Stories by
Anthony Glavin

N E W
ISLAND
BOOKS

THE DRAUGHTSMAN AND THE UNICORN
First published June 1999 by
New Island Books
2 Brookside
Dundrum Road
Dublin 14
Ireland

ISBN 1 902602 06 4

British Library Cataloguing in Publication Data
A catalogue record for this book is available from the British Library

**New Island Books receives financial assistance from The Arts Council
(An Chomhairle Ealaíon), Dublin, Ireland.**

Cover image and design: Jon Berkeley
Typesetting: New Island Books
Printed in Ireland by Colour Books Ltd.

CONTENTS

For Neill, Caitrín and Aoife

SALVAGE

ONLY FOR THE EARTHQUAKE, I would never have heard of Dinny Flynn's death. Though it wasn't a real earthquake, rather a series of tremors beneath the pension where Matt and I were billeted, two Irish exiles in a Nicaraguan rain forest. Behind us, the pension radio interrupted a love song to announce the same subterranean tattoo was troubling the capitol, Managua, ninety miles north. We held our breath, waiting for the other shoe to drop, before Matt ordered two more beers. Casimiro was in bad form—someone had dropped a sweet roll on the pool table, and overnight cockroaches had eaten away a patch of the green felt—but the beers eventually arrived.

As if prompted by our reprieve, Matt started to tell of a letter he got that morning, with news of an Irish schoolmate killed in an automobile accident in Boston. Without knowing why, I interrupted, supplying Dinny Flynn's name. Both Matt and Dinny were from Mayo, but it was the automotive factor that had suddenly brought Flynn to mind.

"You knew him?" Matt shot me a startled glance.

"We worked together a few summers ago in Boston," I replied. The two of us swapped a good few stories about Dinny then, until Father Matt left for bed in the small house beside his tin-fronted church just down from the pension where I was stopping.

I went out for a walk before turning in myself, over the bridge of rusted cables and weathered planks slung across the river. The air beneath the tall intermittent trees along the riverbank was hotter, heavier: a series of muggy pockets in the cooler night. As I neared the airstrip the dark became redolent of some tropical flower: smelling like the lilacs back in Boston. I was only four months in the village, there on a joint Irish–Nicaraguan electrification project, not long enough to name the local flora. Father Matt himself was three years in Nicaragua, hoping for a fourth. Apparently his Irish Bishop was a doctrinal dinosaur, and Matt was in no hurry to be back under his hidebound wing.

"Ireland needs a liberation theology as much as Latin America," Matt often lamented. "But fat chance Rome will allow that, now Franco's dead and Catholic Spain with him in the grave." Though the thought of Franco dead cheered him up a little. No doubt exporting young blood like Father Matt helped keep Ireland an ecclesiastical redoubt back in the Seventies. For my part, I was happy simply to draw my Irish wage packet for helping to light up Nicaragua's revolution.

Dinny Flynn was no Bolshevik, either. And if he once played a fund-raiser for Noraid in South Boston, I suspect for Dinny it was just another gig. An Irish musician wouldn't find much work in Boston without the usual rebel ballads, yet Dinny himself favoured songs about drink, ill-fated love, and other Irish misadventures. He was also mad for Cajun music when I knew him, and getting down to New Orleans was high on his list of get-rich-quick schemes.

I liked the airstrip at night. The jungle was cut back some distance either side, with fewer mosquitoes as a result. The runway was unpaved, fashioned out of crushed stone, but at the far end there was a tiny concrete apron, about ten-foot-square, upon which the ancient DC-3 which flew in daily could position a wheel and effect a 180° turn when wind and weather dictated an easterly take-off. Sometimes I lay down on this concrete patch to gaze up at the unfamiliar stars. Tonight, however, I just turned and taxied the quarter-mile back to the village. Getting into bed, I suddenly thought of my father, who always opened his newspaper to the death notices. "To see which of the lads have given up smoking," he used to quip, though at first I was too young to get the joke. Myself, I only started smoking in Nicaragua, in self-defence against the mosquitoes at Casimiro's. Where Dinny Flynn's obituary had tracked me down, along some seismic telegraph, six months after the fact.

I had met Dinny one summer in Boston, where I was trying to earn enough for the last semester of my electrical engineering degree at Northeastern. Both of us were working room service at a hotel near the Public Gardens. A week after we met, Dinny, who was prone to landlord problems, moved into my Brighton flat. At work we shared an outsized closet, taking phone orders for everything from booze to breakfast. The tips were decent, and it sure beat working on a building site. When things were slow, we might sneak the odd steak up from the kitchen, watching out for Hans, the Austrian Food & Beverage manager, who was a four-star culinary martinet.

And when things were dead slow, we left the phone off the hook and hopped the freight-elevator to the hotel's rooftop terrace, booked mainly for weddings or receptions. Leaning over the rails of the parapet, we would share a joint, staring down at the Boston traffic. Other times Dinny might disappear for an hour, whenever the Puerto Rican chambermaid he was seeing needed help making a bed. Once the three of us were drinking a beer in a suite on the tenth floor, when we saw the door handle turn. Terrified it was the hotel dick—a retired Boston cop named Delaney—Dinny was nearly out on the window ledge before I persuaded him we had the door deadbolted. Easy going, yet excitable, that was Dinny.

Small, fair-haired, and feckless would even better describe him, I suppose. Prior to the hotel, he had worked as a porter at the main branch of the Shawmut Savings Bank. One night his mop handle dislodged the bust of the Shawmut Indian from its lobby pedestal. Dinny swept up the fallen brave and brought a bagful of bits home to glue. Upon discovering another bust of the chief on duty the next night however, he threw the sack into the trash outside his flat. A day later, his supervisor demanded the remains of what had seemingly been the original—nay historical—Shawmut. "For insurance purposes," the boss explained. Working without a Green Card, on a phoney Social Security number, Dinny nipped out for smokes and never went back.

"I might get married and settle down over here," he mused one August evening on the roof of our apartment, where we sometimes went to beat the heat.

"That's one way to get a Green Card," I scoffed, for his matrimonial intentions were as vague as all his pipe dreams. For starters, his Puerto Rican paramour had lately thrown him over for a Boston Red Sox groundskeeper, who slipped her into Fenway Park at night whenever the Sox were out of town, to make love on the outfield grass.

There was usually a breeze on the roof, even the muggiest nights, where we would kill a few quarts of beer. Dinny playing his guitar, and between snatches of Roy Orbison or The Drifters, planning variously for his future. There must have been something in the setting—either the Boston skyline, or the soft underwater glow of the rooftop skylights—that encouraged those nightly variations on the American Dream. Making your fortune was mostly a matter of timing, according to Dinny, who sometimes held off scratching a lottery card for weeks—as if waiting for his luck to catch up with him. A chronic gambler, he told me once how he had every morning bet his boss at a Hyannis motel on the number of drowned moles they would skim off the swimming pool.

While Dinny wasn't lazy, he did feel getting rich shouldn't raise more sweat than unearthing the pot of gold at a rainbow's end. Another rooftop evening he recounted a weekend he had spent in New York, angling for bluefish on Long Island Sound across from LaGuardia. "This coloured guy was lifting every rock along the shore," Dinny enthused. "'Money, man!' he says when I asked him. A plane had gone down the week before, and his buddy had turned up a briefcase with $10,000 in cash!"

"Christ, you sound like my father," I laughed. "Every morning down to the claddagh, hoping something had come in on the tide that would put him on Easy Street forever." Funny enough, I didn't remember then my father's stories of the bodies that washed in during the war, from shipping sunk far out to sea.

In August Dinny dropped all his savings, some $1,500, on a blue, block-long, Oldsmobile Delta 88. A set of wheels was handy for visiting the dog track in Revere, but he could have bought a banger for half that money. I think however Dinny needed something tangible, something as outsized as that Oldsmobile, to show he was truly making it in Amerikay. Maybe the Delta bit even encouraged him he would eventually get down to New Orleans? As for the 88, he played the numbers faithfully with those two fat ladies for the next few months. "Riding along in my Oldsmobile," he lilted as we headed for the Cape one weekend, "My buddy beside me at the wheel." Roll over, Chuck Berry and Beethoven both.

Dinny christened his Olds 'The Bluehound' and pampered it like a pet. America, of course, is car-crazed: auto-part places and petrol stations every fifty yards. Dinny himself was mad for junkyards, always tracking down a used spare-part. I visited a yard with him that November, just after he got sacked from the hotel. For eating a strawberry sundae on the job. Getting fired by Herr Hans hadn't taken a feather out of him, though, and a week later he landed a steady gig at an Irish–American bar near Quincy Market, Tuesday and Thursday nights.

An early snowfall lay on the junkyard, powdering the tiers of tyres and disemboweled engine blocks. Behind the counter in a shed littered with hubcaps was this light-skinned black guy with freckles and ginger hair, who cracked a big grin upon seeing Dinny.

"Yo, Irish, how's the Hound?"

"Meaner than a junkyard dog," countered Dinny, still mourning Jim Croce in a big way.

"Irish needs a starter, Marshall," the black guy instructed his helper, a huge white guy in greasy orange coveralls. Marshall trudged off into the automotive graveyard, returning minutes later like a bird dog, a starter in either hand.

"For you, Irish, thirty-five skins," the black guy smiled at Dinny.

"Look me in the eye and talk to me nicer than that!" protested Dinny, who was probably black himself in a previous life.

"For you, Irish," the junkman grinned, turning his back to Dinny, "thirty-five."

I departed America shortly after I finished my degree, though Dinny wanted me to stay on. By then he had moved into a mansion in Brookline, not far from JFK's birthplace. He had it rent-free, a kind of burglar insurance for the owners who were spending a year abroad. In America, even drifters like Dinny can get by in style. "There's a swimming pool," he coaxed, "a heated garage for Ol' Blue, and more bedrooms than you can count." I moved in for my last month, long enough to suss there was nothing serious about a line I had been doing with a nurse from Milwaukee. Certainly nothing that approximated passionate trespass in moon-lit ball parks or vacant hotel suites.

When my mother wrote at Christmas that my father was ill, I flew back to Ireland. Donegal wasn't what I wanted, but I was happy to be shut of America. Fifty cents at a pet shop near my Brighton flat bought you a goldfish you then fed to the petshop piranha, which lashed about its tank whenever the shop assistant lifted his tiny white net. Even in affluent Brookline there was a similar hint of dog-eat-dog. "Give us this day our Daily Bread," was how my father had always insisted they prayed in the States. "Plus a steak and three eggs."

My father gave up smoking himself a week after I landed home. The night he took what looked a bad turn, I walked in the rain to ring Dr McCabe from a neighbour's house. "Can I get anything?" my mother inquired when McCabe came out of the lower bedroom. "Not much—a sheet, he's dead," replied McCabe, who never had much of a bedside manner. I went down to the claddagh faithfully every morning for a fortnight, before heading to Dublin and an interview with the ESB, who dispatched me to Nicaragua two years later.

As it happened, I couldn't get Dinny out of my head the day after Father Matt gave me the news. We hadn't kept in touch, but there had been something infectious in all that fecklessness. I can't carry a tune in a bucket, yet I found myself humming 'Blue Bayou' that afternoon, one of Dinny's favourites, as I walked back to the village from the small generating station we were constructing on its outskirts. The red clay road lay like a gash through the green underbrush and forest, and some nameless tree was in brilliant yellow flower. Yet I kept seeing Dinny, peering under the Bluehound's bonnet, or studying the racing form at the dog track in Revere, where the lush infield itself looks tropical under the lights at night.

I wrote to his mother in Mayo that night. She wrote back—how Dinny had been playing late, and likely fell asleep at the wheel driving home. In any event The Hound had wrapped itself around a lamppost, the car radio stripped and Dinny's wallet lifted, before the police even arrived. And only then did I remember my father's story of the neighbour who, during the war, had salvaged a gold ring by severing the finger of a sailor washed up on the strand.

The Irish community in Boston had a whip-around to send Dinny home for burial. What's more, his German fiancée accompanied his remains on the flight. I puzzled that one for a while—how marrying a fraulein might net him a Green Card? Still, Dinny had no head for details, and all those love songs he sang probably turned his head anyhow. His mother asked me to visit in Mayo when I got home, but I can picture their place already, boggy meadows all ragwort and rushes, at best a windbreak of stunted pines in front of the cottage. Not Third World but not exactly Europe either: more like Never-Never land in a literal sense.

Yet maybe Mayo explains why Dinny was so utterly seduced by Massachusetts. Childhood is a short season on such rocky ground, whereas America is more like Pinocchio's Pleasure Island. Toy cars to drive down myriad motorways, and a different-flavoured ice cream each day of the year. Certainly he was getting nowhere, Dinny was. Like the winos behind our Brighton flat, who circled the supermarket parking lot in a beat-up Cadillac. Nicaragua meanwhile strikes me as a more honest land. Dozens of yellow butterflies fluttering over a pile of horseshit in the road, the mosquitoes that come out simultaneously with the stars. Mayo and Donegal are less deceptive also, soil barely covering the grey rock beneath.

The night before I left Nicaragua, Father Matt told me of the two Kerry lads shot in a Bronx bar by a Hungarian *émigré*. Apparently there was a row over the respective merits of Ireland and Hungary, neither homeland able to afford them a living. The Hungarian then departed the bar to return with a gun. Shades of 'Stagger Lee', a song Dinny sometimes sang when he got tight. Nationalism, as I mentioned, not being his musical bent.

Blowing out the candle, I got into my canvas cot at the back of Casimiro's pension. There was a big moon out the window, and a breeze off the river was teasing a loose sheet of tin on the roof. Lying there, I kept seeing Dinny's German fiancée in Mayo. Seated in the wake house, shaking hands with an entire parish, puzzling at the chairs lining the walls, the plates of cigarettes, the trays of tea and sandwiches. I keep wondering what in the world she made of Ireland? For that matter, what do I make of this tropical corner, what do any of us make of any land? Meantime, somewhere under the rainbow was a steady job in a junkyard, had Dinny only copped it.

MISSING PERSONS

ALTHOUGH TEN YEARS since Egan had seen Kilcarrick, the village looked little enough changed. The shop boasted an extension, here and there hung Bed & Breakfast signs. A handful of newer bungalows, white pebbledash shining in the late sun, sat like seashells set into the dark green hill. In a way there was less room for change here, Egan realised. Nearly all the scattered dwellings were strung above the narrow road that curved to a halt at the small hotel on the upper arm of the small bay. Below the road, fields fell more or less sharply to the sea. The village proper sat directly above the bay before the road turned toward the hotel: the shop with its Post Office counter, a pair of pubs, a cluster of houses like beads bunched on a string. The sea, always changing, looked of course, utterly the same.

At the elbow of the road Egan turned the car into the lane up to the chalet. "Lobster pots, Davey," he told his three-year-old who asked why there were bird cages piled on the track down to the pier. The pots themselves were a mixture of old and new, orange nylon netting over hazel hoops, a flat stone set in concrete to take them to the bottom. "They look like bird cages, right enough," Egan added when the elder three laughed at the youngest. "What's yellow, weighs five hundred pounds, and sings?" he riddled, hoping to avert tears he saw welling up.

"Oh, Daddy, not again," sounded the chorus from the backseat. Davey beside Egan grinned, too tired from the journey to cry. "See he doesn't head down to the sea alone," Egan cautioned Fiona, the eldest, as he helped Sheila carry their holiday gear inside.

"It's as lovely as ever, Peter," she said fifteen minutes later, standing by the door with an arm around his waist. On the strand below the older children chased, Davey digging in the sand at the high-water mark. Counting the four patches of vivid colour, Egan listened as Sheila told of taking her pupils from the School for the Deaf on an outing to Brittas Bay the year before they married. "It never occurred to me most of them, even at eight or nine, had never seen the ocean before."

"What did they do?"

"They ran headlong into it," Sheila said. "A few fell, absolutely stunned by the wet and cold, but not minding in the least. They were all screaming, as deaf children do, except it sounded different there. Like they were imitating the gulls they couldn't hear."

Sheila went in to prepare their tea, leaving Egan alone outside. Totting up the red, yellow and two blues below, he began to count the gannets falling like cannon-shot far out to sea. Struck by the silence of the scene—heightened somehow by the faint cries from the strand—he puzzled a world with no sound at all.

It was ten years since Egan last saw Kilcarrick, fifteen years since the first time. He had stopped that initial visit at the hotel with his diving partner Moriarty, only a month after they returned from the training course in England. It had been all lakes over there, nothing as wild as this Donegal coast. "We're ahead of the Brits already," Matt remarked as they drove in, making Egan laugh, their apprehension masquerading as bravado. Their first look at the cliffs north of the village however sorted them out in a hurry, no place for chauvinism of any stripe. As they looked down from its height, the sea below looked a single shade of static motionless blue. Working their way down the rock-face to a narrow ledge of flags, they found the water awakened, indeed restless, shifting all black and green at their feet.

They were after a man named McShane who had climbed down after mackerel on a filling tide in the month of August. When he failed to return, several neighbours descended the cliff-face. They found a half-dozen fish on the rock, their emerald hue gone a dark blue, but no sign of McShane. When Egan and Moriarty arrived, the local Guards organized a boat crewed by local fishermen, and the two men dove for three days. They found the fishing rod almost directly below on the seabed, but that was all they found.

It was not all they encountered, however. On the afternoon of the third day, Egan came upon a cavern at the base of the underwater rock. Forty metres below the surface, it lay sixty metres or so north of the ledge where McShane presumably entered the water. Its mouth not much over five metros high, it was easily that wide, and looked deep. The day bright enough to dive without a torch, Egan decided to chance it without ascending for one. He was a few yards into the cave when he saw the shark. It looked over fifteen feet long, himself between it and open water. Rising slowly to the roof of the chamber, Egan drew his knife. It was an instinctive response and idle gesture both, more like hefting a stage prop than weapon, bringing home the absurdity of circumstance. Instantly taking its cue, the shark swam slowly at him, below him, beyond him, its dorsal fin scraping his chest in what seemed almost a benign caress, as Egan fought to remain both horizontal and dead still.

The clarity of the cliffs overhead when he surfaced would remain with him until the day he died. Strangely flat, altogether perpendicular, it seemed there were nothing behind or above them. Until the next day he died, it having felt near enough in that eternity below. Nor did Egan feel himself altogether back in the land of the living, either. Treading water, ignoring the shouts from the boat, he marvelled that a cormorant so steadfast in flight should look so ungainly on a rock to his right, lifting its tail feathers to shit into the sea.

It seemed a strange place, somehow, to suggest for their honeymoon a year later. At first Egan said he had spent a holiday as a child there. He was uneasy, however, at starting married life under false premises, and so told Sheila the truth. "There's no lovelier place with any kind of decent weather," he finished. Sheila saw no reason why they should not spend their week there, his wife nothing if not level-headed herself. Asked what life with a policeman was like, she sometimes answered that never having married a poet or politician, how would she know the difference?

The weather had been more than decent for October, and Sheila too fell for Kilcarrick. They returned twice in the early years, when Fiona and Kieran were still toddlers, renting the same chalet from a local farmer who fished and wove as well. It surprised Egan each visit when the locals placed him perfectly. As if failing to come up with the goods, Moriarty and he had nonetheless earned a certain notoriety. Asking after 'the wee stumpy fellow', they laughed as Egan told how Moriarty had only qualified for the Guards after a friendly sergeant suggested he report early one morning to be measured, having already twice failed the height requirement. "And didn't that extra bit of stretch you have upon awakening finally see him through!"

"You had no problem that way yourself," they told Egan, whose six-feet three-inches had made him and Moriarty something of an odd couple. Shortly after three more lads had joined the Gardai sub-aqua team. Or 'The Apostles' as some wit in Kerry christened them the following year, after they recovered a suspected suicide from a Killarney lake, all of them 'fishers of men'.

Each year when Peter first called to the pub, the locals would carry out a kind of post-mortem on McShane. The majority held that he had suffered a heart attack. Most likely as he cast his line, the momentum taking him into the sea. Had he simply drowned outright they argued, his lungs would have filled with water, body following fishing gear to the bottom. Peter supported this hypothesis, explaining how any air left in the lungs keeps a body buoyant. If only floating five feet off the ocean floor, it would nevertheless follow whatever currents out to sea.

"Like a cork," Doherty, who rented them the chalet, observed.

"Like a cork just," Peter agreed, feeling again an affection for the locals as well as their locale. That McShane was not the sole villager lost at sea likely explained the estimation Egan sensed here for his vocation. It was an appreciation altogether missing in the Midlands town where he was stationed when the recovery team was idle. If the talk in Donegal often turned to drownings it came, Egan felt, more from an awareness of the hunger in a body of water than mere morbidity alone, though not entirely free of that, either. "Great mackerel to be had during the war," somebody would jest as the older men recalled the scavenged bodies that washed onto the strand from ships sunk far out to sea. There were those who had not eaten mackerel since the war, like those who never fancied rabbit after myxomatosis struck, the lanes strewn with their swollen shapes.

No matter how often a story was told, it seemed each time to Egan as if it were being read aloud, such was the fidelity to detail. The coats tied arm-to-arm that had served as a lifeline. The camera found above the cove where a German visitor lost both his footing and his life years before. Occasionally Egan heard confirmed some vague sentiment of his own: of the loneliness to a bog lake that you do not find about the sea. That a drowning is a double tragedy where the remains are not recovered was common knowledge. Other times the odd belief surfaced midst their common wisdom: that the remains of a drowning victim unbalanced in mind always float upon the water. Or, balmy or not, a body always surfaces after nine days. As a rule Egan let such propositions pass unchallenged, accepting it was a country pub, no oracle of any kind. Another story told of a boat who heard laughter as they rowed out one evening after salmon, some of the crew remarking on a strange light that played on the grassy banks above the pier. They saw or heard nothing further, but the following morning the boat failed to return, the sea flat with little wind. "You swallow five hundred organisms in a mouthful of salt water," Doherty instructed Egan, citing as his authority the BBC.

Unlike his inland neighbours, the Kilcarrick men were in a way all trained observers, establishing another bond between them and the visitor. Asking if Egan recalled this or that local, they relied little upon names, describing instead your man's coat, his stature as they had done with Moriarty. Always in a blue cap, or that he walked with a peculiar gait. Most of those in the pub likely knew the registration of every auto in the village, and those like Doherty, who could distinguish among seventy sheep on the hill, impressed Egan with powers of observation a policeman might well envy.

For his part Egan did well with the locals. Unassuming by nature, he was willing to accede to knowledge that, in an isolated village at land's end, seemed more likely to be based on experience than not. Entering into the talk, he often qualified the authority of his own remarks.

"Twelve minutes is as long as a body can remain underwater and still be revived. Or so they say."

"Twelve minutes is a long time," someone responded while the others nodded.

"A lifetime," Egan agreed, thinking of the eternity he had hung suspended between shark and the open sea. He took pains not to suggest anything heroic in that recounting, self-effacing in the description of his fear. On a subsequent visit he failed to mention his promotion to sergeant. The locals learned of it from Gillespie, the local guard. The omission, with its suggestion of modesty, sat well with them.

"You're welcome back," Egan heard this visit also, even if he had failed to bring the good weather with him. Indeed it had rained daily since that first fine evening, though Sheila and he still braved the showers, driving the children out to various sights, the chalet cramped quarters for a family of six. Together they explored sea-caves to the south, to the north the derelict cottages of an isolated fishing townland at the end of a narrow glen. Bits of driftwood, seashells, and oddly shaped pebbles from these outings began to accrue in the chalet, random clusters of flotsam as if the tide crept in and out while they slept. A game of Monopoly that Sheila had packed along with bathing togs occupied Kieran and Mick for hours on end. Davey was happy with games of his own invention, content to wander outside the chalet in his raingear, sometimes inveigling his older brothers down to the strand where he was forbidden to go alone. Fiona, moody these past months as a rule, was herself all clouds and rain, alternately sullen or stormy. There was no jukebox in Kilcarrick, much less a disco; no one her own age that she had met. "I never wanted to come on such a stupid holiday," she repeatedly reminded them.

"We'd have done better to have left her," Peter told Sheila, who replied it was a stage Fiona was going through.

"Are you deaf or what?" Egan shouted at his daughter the following afternoon, patience exhausted. Disdaining to reply, Fiona went out to the car, carrying a rock magazine featuring a band whose multi-coloured coiffure would do a parrot proud.

Shortly after Davey burst into tears, accusing Mick of cheating at a card game he himself was not old enough to follow.

"I think we'll go camping in Brittany next year," Egan fumed. "Huddle in a tent and force-feed them snails and horsemeat pâté."

"Why don't you go down for a pint, Peter, before tea."

"*D'accord*," he offered in parting. The overcast had broken, however, and Egan headed away from the village. He took the path that ran behind the small hotel, which opened only for the summer season. The sun was a red ball over the sea by the time he reached the cliffs, a scattering of raindrops in the grass along the track shining like gems.

As it happened, Egan had avoided the pub after his first evening there. Again he was taken with how little had changed, apart from a new bench beside the fire. There were changes, of course. Conneely, the heavy-set skipper of the fishing boat from which he and Moriarty dove, had died the previous year. Doherty, who rented them the chalet, no longer wove in the loom shed beside his own cottage. "The price of woolen thread has finished it up," the weaver explained.

Still, it struck Egan how slowly life had moved in Kilcarrick, set against his own experience of the intervening years. No longer assigned to the sub-aqua team, Egan had remained in the same Midlands town, which had grown almost as alarmingly as his own family. Though not as bad as what he heard of Dublin, its fabric of community was sorely stretched, threatening to rend at several points. Offences formerly associated with Kojack on TV now showed on the barracks ledger. A week before Egan left on holidays, vandals broke into the church. Smashing the sacristy furniture, they painted its windows alternating panes of red and black. The senseless destruction left Egan more puzzled than angry—no more motive than he had explanation for whatever had transformed his only daughter from sweetheart to contrary stranger almost overnight. No doubt modern times would overtake Kilcarrick, plastic bags already clogging the small stream that tumbled down beside the pier. However there existed yet, for those who gathered nightly in the pub, a continuity of season and memory, a constancy that this summer unsettled Egan, highlighting, as it did, the more erratic flux of his own condition. Formerly a sheltered harbour in which to anchor for a fortnight's time, this season the village resembled more a settlement on the banks of a swiftly moving river, no longer a comfortable port of call.

Egan wondered if there was a raven's nest somewhere on the cliff, a pair of them protesting loudly as they circled his descent, their bodies oddly magnified against the hazy sky. Moving slowly down, he leaned into the rockface whenever he had to lunge or drop. It took several minutes, but he reached the ledge of flagstones without incident, out of breath since he was out of shape. Moving carefully to the water's edge, he noted how the rock turned two-toned where the wash lapped the barnacle-encrusted shelf. Among the crevasses were pockets of mussels he had initially thought would make great eating in another year's time. According to the locals, though, they never matured to any size, sole survivors of Tir na nÓg.

Egan stared into the water, noting the small flags of dulse that waved gently as the rock sloped away. He saw nothing more, and nothing untoward would happen either. Life, unlike the telly, does not lay on melodrama daily. No shark's fin cut the placid surface, only a red buoy that bobbed above a lobster pot. In the pub this visit they had spoken only briefly of McShane. Doherty recalled the three days of diving, "as calm as came before or since", sounding as if the fine weather had been the previous week. While the locals seemed willing to let the incident lie, Egan had found himself thinking more about the missing man—as if the file on McShane had yet to close. Ideal company for a holiday, he mused—a man fifteen years dead, whose face you never knew, whose family you never met.

He squatted down by the water's edge, thinking how often he had heard it said that it did not do to go down to the sea alone. The wonder was that he could feel so alone, nearly a fortnight in Doherty's matchbox of a holiday home. Glancing up, Egan wondered at having climbed down at all, at what he had hoped to find. Like a criminal returning to the scene, only there had been no crime. No foul play suspected, unless it were a violation of God's law.

"If you fell in there, you'd be done for," McShane had told Doherty earlier on that long-ago August afternoon, indicating the depth below the pier on which the two men stood. Premeditation or precognition, the end result had been much the same. As a gull cried overhead, Egan thought of that childhood conundrum—whether a gun discharged in the desert makes a retort, if there is nobody there to hear it? When you die unwitnessed and unwaked however, you are no less dead for that.

That first August Doherty told Egan of an uncle who recovered the body of an English sailor lost at sea. Somehow managing to haul the remains up a steep bank, he had carried the drowned man three miles into Kilcarrick. For years after the family in Yorkshire sent a sum of money at Christmas out of gratitude.

"You had more than one out then," Conneely cut in, "eyeing the rocks."

"No shortage of bodies during a war," smiled Doherty. "Though they don't bring the same price as in peacetime."

"Sure, isn't your man here," Conneely indicated Egan, "paid to do that very job."

And if, as the poet suggests, you become what you contemplate, perhaps this melancholy holiday was only a post-dated draft for his years of diving after the missing and the dead. Either way, whatever he had expected to find on these flags, he was left with nothing more than surface and integument, a faint breeze wrinkling the skin of the water in haphazard patterns. Rising to his feet, he spat gently into the sea, watched as his spit spread slowly like a miniature wreath upon the deep. He was halfway up the cliff when a pebble glanced off a rock beside his head. Peering up, he saw Sheila peering down.

"I was about to send out a search party, Peter."

"How did you know to find me here?"

"Fiona saw you heading in this direction."

"Nice of her to let on," he laughed.

She handed him a small bouquet of meadowsweet, taking his hand as they walked back to the village. Feeling the warmth of her bare arm against his own, he thought again of McShane who had never married, who had lived and died alone. Sheila and he who had not made love this holiday in the shrunken chalet, had done little else that first October long ago. If their years between had witnessed every kind of ebb and flow, he sensed this evening a kind of current that might carry him yet.

Supper eaten, they left Fiona in charge of the younger three. Egan suggested the hotel lounge, but Sheila said she would prefer the pub. Whether it was her presence or not, the talk this time seemed gentler, almost fanciful. Yarns of a villager who left his bed asleep, descended the cliffs to rob the nests there. Come morning, the speckled eggs on the kitchen dresser were the only clue the family had to his wandering. The following night they secured the latch from within, whereupon the somnambulist awoke the household by dragging the table across the kitchen flags, as if he were hauling a boat above the tide.

"They're living in the past, aren't they, Peter?" Sheila asked as they walked back to the chalet.

"To a degree, I suppose," Egan agreed. "Though at less risk, perhaps, where it still seems near enough."

They piled into the car that next afternoon for the trip home, Fiona asking could she listen to the Top Twenty. "OK but it's not to play too loudly," Egan said. Generally he preferred the radio off, a surfeit of noise from the kids as it was. His eldest had come momentarily out of her sulks, however, and he was not unwilling to accommodate her. "You're tops, Pops," Fiona quipped, rewarding him in turn with a flash of her old affection.

As they drove the narrow road that rose from the village, Egan heard the lyric repeat itself, a throaty female vocalist, longing to die in a sea of love. It was the kind of conjunction that occurs with some frequency he had observed over the years. Every so often such circumstance even offered itself to his line of work. "It's that strange bit of luck you learn to watch out for, like a shiny dime on the sidewalk." Or so said a Boston detective whom Egan had met on holiday in Ireland once. As the song played on, Egan turned for a last look at the sea, lying like a lover in the arms of the bay. If not fighting it so much now, feeling once again that he hadn't a clue.

PIRANHA

NOW THAT THEY no longer went to The Casket, Mick and Mary sometimes had a sit-down Chinese in Killester instead. It was there Mick got the reminder, as if one were needed, after his pork foo yung one Saturday night. "Tell me about it," he said, handing Mary the tiny slip of paper.

"*A joke's a very serious thing*," Mary winced. "Some bloody fortune, six months too late."

"Maybe they got a good deal on Chinese hindsight cookies," Mick said. "What's yours?"

"*Don't let your tongue cut your throat*," Mary read aloud.

"That one must have been Terry's fortune so," Mick winced in turn.

"Things weren't so hot between him and Paula anyhow."

"Well, we didn't help, did we?"

"Will you stop," Mary said, pushing back her chair. "How about we go for an Indian next Saturday?"

On the way home Mick told Mary about another practical joke that had not gone so badly. In an Indian take-away in London years before, where his mate Fergal had noticed this fat unshaven bloke in a wrinkled blue suit asleep at a table in the corner. Borrowing a biro off the girl at the till, Fergal scribbled something on a scrap of paper and tucked it into the man's breast pocket.

"What did you write?" Mick asked outside.

"That he's been slipped a magic love potion," Fergal said, "and women won't be able to resist him once he wakes." What Mick really admired was 'love potion'—something he'd have never come up with himself. That had been a class joke all right—compared to the stunt the gang had pulled on Terry Delaney six months ago.

The Lotto gag on Terry had been Anto and Ali's idea, but Mick and Mary had gone along regardless. The same Anto and Ali, who along with Mick and Mary, plus Terry and Paula, made up the Gang of Six which met at The Casket Saturday nights. The pub was nominally Kelly's, but there had been a shop, The Casket, attached to it, and the name followed the pub even after young Kelly converted the shop into an off-licence after the old man died.

All of the gang had grown up in the same part of Dublin's Northside. Attended the same National school, the same dances at The Blind in Drumcondra and so on. Now in their early forties, they had come of age in the Seventies, done some drugs—hash, grass, bennies—and in Anto Murphy's case a few tabs of acid. Drink however had been—and remained—the drug of choice. Three or four times a year now the girls got together at Paula's house with a few bottles of wine, but The Casket on Saturday nights was the main event.

Not that The Casket is much to write home about. Just another Northside local where you can cut the cigarette smoke with a blunt knife by half-nine most nights, though the smoke at least helps mask the whiff from the jacks at the side door. Of course the regulars notice neither smoke nor smell, and odds are mostly only regulars drink there. Not that The Casket's vibe differs from most Dublin locals towards outsiders—an initial open appraisal followed by an indifference tinged with just enough hostility to establish the fact of territory.

Mick was the only one of the lads who had ever left Dublin. To work on the sites in London for a few years, before coming back and taking up where he and Mary had left off. Two years later they married, first of the three couples to get hitched. For a while Mick worked washing windows, except for Tuesdays when he signed on. Until one morning Gay Byrne mentioned on radio a Southside scam where window-washers were falling off ladders and suing houseowners, most of whom weren't covered for personal liability. The next week half his regulars turned Mick away at the door. However Mary, who was pregnant, had been at him to get something better anyhow, and a month later Mick was delivering milk. Rising at three a.m. every morning, and no longer signing on. The first winter was hard-going, but gradually Mick grew to like the work, seeing the sun come up on good days, driving along the quiet streets.

The change in employment didn't pass Anto by, though that hardly bothered Mick who had grown up across the road from Murphy's mouth.

"You getting any more as a milkman," he leered, "than you did washing windows?"

"Not half what you taximen get," Mick said. "So feck off, Murphy."

There was always something a bit edgy about Anto and sex, and he had a new scruffy joke every Saturday night. His Ali paid him no mind, but Mick's Mary was not that gone on Anto.

"He fancies himself," she told Mick one night after the pub. "Trying to look the young fellah, sideburns and Chelsea boots."

"Ah Anto's all right."

"He gives me the willies sometimes."

"Oh, he'd give you his willy quick enough," Mick grinned.

"Will you feck off!"

"You think it's true?" Mick asked. "What Paula's sister said about his thumb?"

"How's that?" Mary asked.

"That it hadn't a nail?"

"Oh, stop!" Mary reached for her toothbrush. The story was Anto had walked Paula's younger sister Helen home from a dance when they were in school. It was a frosty night, so Anto told Helen to put her hand inside the pocket of his trench coat, where she clasped what she thought was Anto's thumb, until she suddenly realised it had no nail.

Even if Anto had sex on the brain, Mick found him good crack, full of stories from his twelve-hour taxi-shifts, like the fare who claimed he was into astral travel.

"'I used to suffer from asthma myself,' I tell him."

"'No, I'm serious,' the guy goes. 'Astral travel—like when you move around outside your body.'"

"'So why the fuck,' I ask him, 'are you taking a cab?'"

Anto was full of schemes too when he wasn't behind the wheel. Like selling used motors for a Coolock garage out of his driveway—placing an ad in *The Evening Herald* and posing as the owner. His Ali, who had the use of them between sales, did her shopping in a Volvo one week and in a Mercedes the next.

Stories, schemes, and jokes—that was Anto. But if Anto loved a practical joke, Ali was nearly as bad. Like the time Caroline, who worked in the same insurance office on Dorset Street, complained about a stale cake from Bewley's.

"Return it," Ali told her.

"Oh, I wouldn't do that," Caroline said.

"I'll do it for you," said Ali, who cut the Bewley's label off a pack of tea at home. A week later Caroline got what looked like an apology from Bewley's, instructing her to present the letter for a free cake at any branch. Caroline took the letter into Grafton Street and got a fresh cake, no bother. Delighted, she thanked Ali, who promptly showed her the Bewley's label taped to a blank A4 sheet she had then photocopied before typing the letter herself. Caroline was not amused however, and relations soured afterwards.

"Feck her if she can't take a joke," said Anto, who used to leave a banger inside the geyser above the kitchen sink at the flat he and Terry shared years ago on the North Circular Road. First up, Terry would run the hot water before shaving and be blown out of his socks. After a few weeks he would forget to check the geyser, and Anto would strike again.

The stunt Anto pulled after Mick came back from London was a different kettle of fish however. A tank of tropical fish, to be precise, which Mick installed in the flat shortly after he moved in with the other two. Into fish since he was a kid, Mick had long since graduated from guppies and goldfish to Harlequins and Neon Tetras. Noting how fond Mick was of them, Anto bought a half-dozen goldfish in a pet shop on Capel Street and, in a separate plastic bag, a small piranha. Back at the flat he scooped Mick's fish into a saucepan of water. He waited then until he heard footsteps on the stairs, before emptying both plastic bags into the tank. The water looked to be boiling as Mick came through the door, but the frenzy had ceased by the time he reached the tank, the piranha cruising among a few crimson shreds. Bursting into tears, Mick grabbed a heavy glass ashtray and went for Anto, but Terry got in between them, shouting at Mick it was only a joke.

Terry, the third lad, had grown up around the corner from Mick and Anto. Short, heavyset, he had worn his hair long through the Seventies, but what little was left was now all short, back and sides. The second to marry, after he got Paula pregnant, Terry was the only one with a permanent and pensionable gig: nearly twenty years now selling stamps behind a hatch at the GPO. Moody, sometimes sullen, he was mad for the ponies and his golf game, only he never talked of them. Or much else, for that matter. 'The Mystery Man,' Anto had taken to calling him behind his back.

The gang saw less of one another once they married. Until their kids—two in each family—got older, and they could get out without a babysitter. Saturday nights at The Casket, which started around then, included Paula's sister Helen at first, until her marriage broke up and Helen dropped out. For the others however, The Casket became what you did on a Saturday night. Plus the odd week-night, if there was a table quiz for the school or the Scouts.

It had been the same old song for nearly a decade now, but only over the last year had Mick found himself not always looking forward to Saturday night. Listening to Anto run his mouth about Man United or Terry and his Paula bitching at each other. Sometimes he thought of following Liverpool or Chelsea just to annoy Anto, but in fact he didn't give a feck about the Premiership.

"It's your mid-life crisis," Mary joked one night, after Mick said something about feeling there was a hole in his life. Mary had the kids to keep her going in a way he didn't however, and Mick said nothing more at home. Two weeks later he saw an ad in *The Northsider* for saxophone lessons. The teacher, Jack, turned out to be a bloke his own age, with a spare sax Mick could hire until he was ready to buy one. Mick thought the lessons were going OK, but after three or four of them Jack announced he was emigrating to Australia in a fortnight. Two months later, Mick saw Jack in the carpark at the Northside Shopping Centre. "How's life down under, you bollix?" Mick wanted to shout, but didn't.

Sometimes Mick thought it was maybe Dublin that had changed—not himself. Like the colours had washed out of the city, leaving it a drabber, harsher place, even if the place was awash in money the last few years. More people driving late-model cars, and half the crowd at the Casket packing a mobile phone on their hips as they crowded up to the bar for last orders on Saturday nights. Even Anto's stories had more of an edge now, the astral travellers replaced by more malevolent spiders from Mars. Like Merno, who rang on a mobile phone one night about a BMW Anto was selling.

"I answer the phone," Anto told them in the pub, "and this voice goes, 'This is Merno', like he doesn't know what to say next."

"'What's up, Merno?' I say."

"'I could be interested in that car.'"

So Anto wrote down an address in Neilstown. Unsure of the territory, he asked another taxi-man, Larry, who knew the west of the city cold.

"It's like Beruit in there," Larry told him. "You'd be mad to drive a Beamer in."

Anto found the house that afternoon, plywood over an upstairs window, a burnt-out Subaru in the next drive. Merno answered the door, a short skinny scanger, about twenty-five.

"In jeans and a white shirt," Anto told the gang, "covered with tatts, *Love & Hate* across his knuckles, the works."

Anto followed him into the sitting room, empty except for a busted sofa, the remains of a Chinese carry-out, and a couple of empty cider cans.

"So what do I do now?" Merno asked.

"Do you want to drive it?" Anto asked.

"I don't drive."

"You want to get somebody to drive it?"

"No, I trust you."

"That's all right."

"So what do I do next?"

"I'm asking £9,250," Anto said, figuring he can get 8,500.

Only Merno just said, "OK."

"So do you want to buy it?"

"Yeah."

"OK," said Anto, having finally figured out the rhythm.

"So what do I do next?"

"Pay me."

"Cash OK?"

"Perfect."

But as Merno slid a briefcase out from under the sofa, Anto suddenly remembered from a hundred movies how the pay-off inside the case, purse or paperbag is always a gun, never the spondoolicks. As his gut tightened, he looked behind at the door. When he turned around however, Merno was peeling notes off a thick wad of fifties like he was dealing from a deck of cards.

"How did you get home?" Mary asked in the pub.

"I rang Larry on my mobile to collect me in his taxi," Anto finished his pint.

"No wonder Merno likes his Chinese take-away," Terry said. "Being in the laundry business."

"You were lucky to get out unscalped," Paula shook her head at Anto.

"I got him to change the mobile number," Ali said. "As I didn't fancy Merno ringing back how one of the tyres was bald or something."

"Or offering to check your oil," Anto laughed.

"Give it a rest, dipstick," Ali said.

Not long after, Anto and Ali proposed the Lotto joke on Terry. A serious Chinese-fortune-cookie kind of joke. For years the gang had played the same Quick-Pick Lotto numbers. Styling themselves the Syndicate of Six, describing how they would splash out if they hit it big. Sun holidays in Mexico or a new house in Howth, since no one wanted to live alongside the wankers and rock stars in Dalkey or Killiney.

"Shit, I'd settle for a refrigerated van," Mick said, getting a laugh.

"I'd get an extra hour's sleep," he elaborated, "if I could load up the night before."

"You could lie in till noon if you won, eejit," Anto said.

"I won't sell another bleeding stamp anyhow," Terry said.

Then, around the time Mick started his sax lessons, Terry dropped out of the syndicate. "I want to play my own numbers," he informed the gang.

"You won't see tuppence of my share," Paula told him, "if the rest of us win."

"Nor you mine, Sweetheart," Terry said, none too sweetly.

Shortly after, Terry started coming into The Casket a half-hour late, after the winning numbers were announced on the TV. A few months later Anto got his bright idea.

"We give him the winning numbers," he told the others. "Only they'll be his own."

"We couldn't do that!" Mick's Mary protested.

"Why not?" Anto said.

"How'll you get the numbers?" Mick asked.

"You can get them?" Anto looked at Paula.

"Ah, no," Paula said. "I'm not setting myself up for that."

"We're setting him up, you eejit!"

"You don't have to go home with him, Anto, after he learns he didn't win."

Anto kept after her for weeks, but Paula kept saying no, until the night of the Scouts table quiz. Mick and Mary couldn't make it, but the other four had made up a team. A table of secondary-school teachers in the corner were eight points ahead after five rounds, but that didn't stop Terry from digging into Paula for having insisted Kansas City was the capital of Kansas.

"You stupid cow."

"Fuck you," Paula said, only Ali could see her eyes begin to fill.

"I'll give you that bastard's numbers Saturday," Paula told Anto when Terry went off to the jacks. "He leaves the slip on the telephone table every Thursday night."

"Good on ya," Anto said. "The Jackpot's over two million this week."

"Two, seven, twelve, seventeen, twenty-eight and thirty-two," Paula told Anto on the Saturday.

"Jaysus, he'll never win with those numbers," Mick said, writing them on a beer mat.

"He wins tonight anyhow!" Anto laughed, jotting them down also. "We wait till he asks what the numbers were, right?"

Terry arrived a full hour later. His hair wet like he'd had a shower, and in good form for once.

"You're all picture and no sound," he told Paula who had gone quiet, but there was no barb in it. He didn't ask about the Lotto though, until the lights flashed for last orders. Then, as if reminded, "Anybody get the numbers?"

"Ah, feck the numbers," Mick said, flipping Terry a beer mat.

"Oh you wrote them too?" Anto said, casual like, passing Terry the other mat before carrying on with a story about three German tourists in his taxi. The rest of the gang ignored Terry, who looked at both beer mats, before tossing them onto the table where he kept glancing at them. He said nothing but Mary, seated across, could see he had gone all white.

When Mick stood for the last round, Terry got up too and headed for the jacks. When Mick got back to the table, Anto and Ali were grinning like kids, while Paula looked like she might throw up.

"We'd better tell him it's a joke," Mary said as Mick sat down.

"Ah let him enjoy his millions for a few minutes more," Anto laughed.

It was another five minutes before Terry come out of the jacks. The colour was back in his face, flushed now as if he'd been jogging. He did not sit down when he reached them either. Instead, standing over the table, he threw a set of keys down in front of Paula.

"You can have the house and car," he told her. "And I've been sleeping with your sister Helen for a year." Waving at them, he turned and walked out of the pub.

Mick watched Terry go out the door, then turned back to the table where Paula sat, face frozen, staring at a stain on the floral carpet. His own Mary had her face in her hands, crying, while Ali looked like it was her turn to be sick. To his right he could hear Anto whispering "Fuck me, fuck me, fuck me"—like a mantra to make it all right again.

The bar was shut now and the lights on full: the unrelenting brightness like an operating theatre. Or a cinema after the credits finish rolling. Only Mick knew this was no movie, no way to rewind the reel, cut and splice for a happier ending. Looking down at the table, he took in the overflowing ashtray and puddles of spilled drink, a red pack of Carrolls, a blue-foil peanut bag, a lime-green crumpled crisps packet. All the colourful wreckage of their Saturday night friendships, shimmering like the bits and bobs of what he had mistaken for his Red Phantoms and Blue Gouramis, floating on top of that long-ago tank.

HEALTH, MONEY & LOVE

THE BIRD WAS at the window again, small beak striking the pane, wings beating the stone sill in its frenzy. It drew Rodney, already awake, from his bed, but flew off as he drew the curtains. He sensed it would return once he left the room, as it had done the night before when he first heard its tiny commotion from the sitting room. He often heard gulls on the roof, scrabbling over the tiles, but this noise had been more a miniature tattoo; a muted rustling such as feminine garb formerly made.

Standing in the first light, he noted its droppings along the window ledge, patterned like some cryptic calligraphy for him to decipher. Did the bird portend? Might Sally answer him that? It looked a kind of wren, small and undistinguished, though he was no bird-fancier. The African joopoe that excited many of the English on Majorca appeared to his eye little more than a smaller magpie with a touch of red. The nightingale was less a disappointment—though he had been disappointed this year, leaving it until the previous week to walk out below the village in search of its song. Late June was late in the year, however, and he had heard only a few scattered notes from a lone bird, the cicadas loud in the fading light.

The bedside clock showed nearly six, an hour before rising time. Awake most mornings by five, Rodney preferred to lie on than get up with nothing to do. It was generally a quiet time at least, too early for the odd lorry along the unpaved road beside his house. When Rodney first arrived seven years before, there had been scarcely a car in the village, the only traffic past his dwelling the donkey-drawn carts with their large wooden wheels. Oddly enough the small carts made almost as much noise as a lorry: the iron-rimmed wheels as they grated on the road echoed in every stone of his bedroom wall. It was one of these carts that had finished sleep this morning, shortly before the bird appeared.

Seeing nothing for it but to get up, Rodney rose. He would sweep the sitting room floor, thereby delaying breakfast until its customary hour. "Aren't most of life's pleasures a matter of hitting yourself over the head so that you can stop?" Rodney proposed on evenings when he allowed himself a second gin & tonic. Not eating in order to eat, not drinking in order to drink. After three years of this regimen, Rosalyn had returned to London, to write Rodney there was more to life than an intermittent headache. Happy to be nearer her daughters from a previous marriage, she added that she loved him, and hoped he would join her there. In April he had flown to England for a month. Rosalyn was his third wife, and he was seventy years old. "Women like to cuddle, don't they, and you find yourself being edged out of the bed," he spoke from experience whenever the subject of matrimony arose.

Bracken, who showed no surprise at seeing Rodney up, saw no reason why its own breakfast need be postponed. The Wilsons, English friends in a nearby village, had asked Rodney to take on the cat after its owner, their neighbour, departed the island, leaving the animal to fend for itself. The Wilsons already had two dogs and a cat. Large and tawny, Bracken was hopelessly insecure. Eager for Rodney's lap, it insisted on kneading his knees until its claws snared his trousers, ensuring that he would fling it down. As if by courting rejection in small doses, it might ward off another outright desertion at a later date. Rodney suspected it had been taken from its mother too soon. Else ruined by its previous master, allowed to clamber up his surplice or something. Rodney had never met the man, a homosexual minister according to the Wilsons, transferred to Tunisia. Heeding the adage it is better to annoy small children and animals than outright ignore, he tossed an occasional pebble at Bracken dozing in the garden.

The cat fed, Rodney fed himself. Breakfast was a boiled egg, large slice of bread, two cups of coffee, a small rasher every second day, though the meat wasn't up to much. Ideally you wanted to be an alcoholic vegetarian on Majorca, where both liquor and greens were cheap. A bowl of soup followed at one, tea at quarter-to-four, dinner at seven. "Not painting so much as dining by numbers!" quipped his lodger Morris, artist-in-residence, the month before. The meals—bracketed by their preparation and washing up—served to eat up a great deal of the day. In Rhodesia Rodney had found that temptation in the bush had consisted almost solely of anticipating your food; the danger being that you found yourself sitting down to supper at ten in the morning. Now, for all his regimented Majorcan mealtimes, Rodney ate very little. Death enters through the stomach, or so the Japanese held, Rodney nothing if not catholic in his maxims. "Nothing too much," he often advised Rosalyn, echoing the oracle of old.

Satisfied it had cooled, he took the dishwater out to the honeysuckle planted upon his return from London, entering the garden via the French doors in the dining room. The garden was laid out like a cart wheel, pebbled paths radiating like spokes from the small hub of gravel beneath a pair of pomegranate trees. The house itself sat on the absolute edge of the village. To the west, beyond the garden's wire fence, was an almond orchard. Beyond that, the flat countryside stretched some five kilometres to small mountains stippled with pines. To Rodney the mountains seemed to obtrude or recede depending upon the light. In winter with clouds or rain they loomed like something glimpsed at sea. The sea itself lay twenty kilometres north, visible from the village plaza, no great distance for the gulls that walked his roof.

From the garden Rodney saw it would be another fine day, the sky that remarkable Mediterranean blue, not a cloud in sight. At bedtime the night before the glass had fallen slightly. Waking a few hours later, he had arisen and gone outdoors to urinate, noting a darker shade to the road before he felt the wet on his arms, the rain coming down like a thief in the night, the ground so dry it drank up any sound as well. It had been a brief shower, enough only to lay the dust. When the good weather held for weeks, any daily variables lay with the wind or the neighbour women. In bright sun the mistral hard from the west resembled more a current of light than air. This morning, though, the wind was from the east; and as yet no sign of life from the houses beyond his eastern garden wall. There were weeks when the women shouted at one another from morning to night; less often there were days of silence. One family kept a dog tied to a tree at the bottom of their garden. On days when the dog added its voice to the clamour, Rodney would shout at the women in English to shut up, believing they would think he was yelling at the dog. The women would hush so; leaving the dog, bored by its confinement, to carry on.

It was pointless to talk of mistreating animals to the locals; the Wilsons had, only to be informed that at least Majorcans didn't beat their *children*. Not that such had been Rodney's childhood experience. His mother had opted to ignore rather than annoy or abuse, packing him off at age five from their large house in Co Wicklow, Ireland to a series of English monastery schools. Sixty years later, his abiding memory was of never having had enough to eat. Still the Majorcan manner with dumb beasts was a source of confusion and exasperation. Once Rosalyn and he had rescued a dog with a front paw caught in its collar. Watching the four-footed animal immediately play havoc with a field of sheep, they gathered its entanglement had been a deliberate hobbling.

Later Rodney had seen dogs used in this fashion to gather sheep, limping along on three legs. "Too bloody lazy to train them properly," he fumed. That he had taken Bracken for a distemper shot proved the talk of the village, nobody having ever visited the vet with a cat before. Worst were the thrushes which the locals trapped in nets by the thousands. "I can't imagine what pleasure there is in eating such a small bird," Rodney had remarked to the postman, encountering only consensus from the Majorcan, who suggested you needed to eat as many as twenty-four. "I suppose they've drawn the line at shooting nightingales," Rodney remarked afterwards to Rosalyn.

The bird that morning at his window he forgot, until he discovered the roses gathered after breakfast for the sitting room were alive with earwigs. Not as a rule squeamish, Rodney found the dark beetles darting among the petals entirely unsettling, his unease reminding him then of the bird frantic to enter his bedroom. He thought again of Sally—odd that he should, though, as he considered her a charlatan. A self-described clairvoyant, Sally assured Rodney she had been run ragged with readings in England. By day in the shopfront she shared with an Indian peddling joss-sticks and the odd waterpipe, and evenings at home. "I gave good value for three quid," Sally explained. "Cups, cards, and Spiritual Guidance if someone was troubled." Most of her clientele however opted for a straight fortune, a biscuit or two laid on with the tea. As you could get only tea-bags in the village, Sally now sent to England for the loose leaves she divined.

His nearest English neighbours, Sally and Roger lived a mile down the road to the Caves which were the village's sole tourist attraction. Just six months on Majorca, they were refurbishing a small ranch with scant funds and even less *Español,* whatever about *Mallorquin.* Rodney had taken them under his wing to a degree, though he found them somewhat pathetic, their company tedious after a half-hour. They seemed a feckless pair, constantly being done by the locals, beset by one minor catastrophe after another. A carpenter by trade, Roger was to the authorities first and foremost a foreigner, thereby ineligible for a work permit. Several years short of his pension, he managed a few odd jobs on the side.

For her part Sally was constrained more by the Church than State, reluctant to post a notice at the Caves which she felt certain would both attract a brisk trade and give offence. In the meantime Rodney had brought a few people down to her. They seemed well-pleased, though to his mind anybody who sought a reading was likely to be satisfied—the entire undertaking a self-fulfilling proposition, whatever about prophecy. Still, 'charlatan' was a bit harsh, in that he believed Sally sincere, if mistaken, about her powers. She was impressive enough reading cups: descrying sums of money, weddings and funerals as if they appeared before her eyes. However the 'fortunes' revealed by her 'three guides' were another matter. Seated without ceremony at her kitchen table, she transcribed directly into a red jotter, more secretarial than sibylline. Heavy-set with untidy hair, she sometimes sat troubled by gas, only moments after receiving messages from the other side.

Rodney had suggested to her that trade would likely remain slow. Most of the English on the island were elderly; not having much future, they probably were not pushed to hear about it. Moreover the majority might find the clairvoyant and carpenter common. The issue of class was also compounded by a question of shared experience. Whereas his nearest English neighbours knew only Britain, Birmingham no less, most of their compatriots had landed on Majorca from farther afield: Kenya, India, Kuala Lumpur. "The residue of empires," Rodney once described them to Morris, so delighting his American lodger that Rodney now trotted out the epigram from time to time. It included himself, of course; four years in Rhodesia studying citrus management, followed by more than twenty years in Brazil, overseeing 30,000 grapefruit trees on a coastal farm south of Santos.

For all their limitations, Rodney saw Sally and Roger once a week. Born in Ireland of old Anglo-Irish stock newly converted to Catholicism, Rodney had been raised among the memories of a monied class. Shuttled between England and Ireland on school holidays, he had grown up feeling, on various continents, that he didn't quite fit—all of which tempered his response to the Birmingham pair. And so once a month he had them to breakfast on the balcony above the garden, accepting that not everybody was as able for solitude as he. The German widow who sold him the house had evidently drunk a good deal, startling the neighbour women with loud peals of laughter from the upper rooms in which she never entertained and seldom left. During his first year on Majorca, Rodney had gone months without speaking English, any conversation limited to a few Spanish phrases in the shop, the reflection of his lathered visage as he shaved in the bathroom as much company as he might see for weeks. Even now he was without a confidant among the locals, the language problem and his shyness compounded by his belief that peasants were unable to think in the abstract, a handicap which limited any conversation before it commenced.

After a year in the village, Rodney met the Wilsons at the Caves. Seldom in the plaza bars, he occasionally walked down to the terraced café set into the limestone hill that housed the caves themselves. All bougainvillea and potted hydrangea, its handful of tables beneath a pitched pine roof overlooked a series of low hills beyond the road with its belt of cypress trees. While neither a big smoke nor city lights, it nonetheless afforded a possible chat with tourists, the outside chance of a single woman. Besides, you took what opportunities there were, as Rodney had learned long ago. Every so often in Brazil a mailboat had replaced the freighters that moored offshore to onload fruit from barges alongside. Were it your turn among the managers to supervise, you took advantage of a better class of boat. Attended by a steward, you had a meal with wine on board, a taste of civilised life.

Spying the Wilsons one afternoon at a corner table, Rodney had asked might he join them, attracted as much by the lovely girl in their party as by their native tongue. The young woman turned out to be a niece on holiday, the Wilsons permanent residents on the island. Hearing something of his life in the house beyond the hills, the niece suddenly asked Rodney if he were happy? The older man was taken aback by the tactless query— almost rude, for all her delicate features and flaxen hair. It sounded the kind of thing an American might ask, for surely you don't go into why you are unhappy among strangers in an open-air café. Reflecting later, Rodney decided for true happiness you needed to be both in love *and* solvent. Rarely, if ever, had he known the two together.

The niece was returning to Bath that night, but the Wilsons had invited Rodney to tea the Sunday following, after which they began to see one another regularly. Robert and Kay were several years on Majorca, revolution and unrest having routed them from Cyprus and Tanzania, where they had previously settled upon Robert's retirement as a pilot for a mining concern with holdings throughout East Africa. Forty years out of the United Kingdom, Kay dreaded the right-hand drive in Spain, accustomed to the English side of the road in the former colonies. She and Robert were in poor health; after lunch at Rodney's they generally took a nap in his guest bedroom off the sitting room. Upon rising, they all took tea in the garden, where the Wilsons complained about the soaring cost of everything, of their loneliness. If they had his sympathy on inflation, Rodney had little patience on the latter score. "The problem with Robert and Kay," he informed Rosalyn, "is that they are not self-sufficient."

Through them Rodney met Gordon, who rounded out his small circle of acquaintances. "A committed theosophist" as Kay

Wilson described him, Gordon was also an artist. Bent with rheumatism, he had called on Rodney attired in jacket and ascot, outsized eyes set above a long nose that shaded a salt and pepper goatee. After changing from shorts into trousers, Rodney broke out a tin of inferior Majorcan pork pâté which he served in a porcelain Fortnum & Mason's jar. However conversation with Gordon proved livelier than with the Wilsons. Talk of ectoplasm, reincarnation or speculation of another dimension from whence UFOs possibly materialised. The pair of them also swapped stories of Rhodesia where Gordon too had lived, and stories of Ireland where the painter had spent childhood summers on the estate of a great-uncle outside Limerick.

"He told us of the fairies who talked to him."

"'What did they say, Uncle?' we'd ask him."

"'Oh, I can't say what, because they always spoke in Irish!'"

Of Gordon's work, Rodney had seen nothing to date. The Wilsons said he was highly regarded in Rhodesia, a painting hung in its Royal Academy no less. Of his past, Rodney learned little more. That there had been a wife he gathered one afternoon over a third gin & tonic. Upon leading Gordon into the garden, Rodney saw to his chagrin his laundered sheets still hanging on the line from lemon to pomegranate tree. "It's only dirty linen that one mustn't air in public," Gordon assured him, dismissing his apologies. Deaf to his own precept, he proceeded to tell Rodney that, not until they married, had his wife informed him that she was unable to bear children.

"I slapped her across the face," he concluded. Had Rodney ever wanted children? he then inquired.

"I'm afraid I've spent most of my time and some money avoiding them," Rodney replied, noting the silhouette of a rose bush trailing along a bedsheet like shadow-play on an empty cinema screen. "For years I could barely afford to keep myself."

"Yet they say if you have them, you do end up providing for them," Gordon observed, bending to retrieve his cane which Bracken had dislodged from the tea-table. The dust raised by a tractor tilling the nearby orchard seemed of a piece with the fading sunlight as it drifted into the garden. Steering the chat back to Ireland, Rodney told of his grandfather at church one Sunday. "Who are those women?" he inquired of the seven girls wearing white in the family pews. "Your daughters," the old man was duly informed.

Once the honeysuckle was watered, Rodney sat down to finish a letter begun the previous evening. It was to Rosalyn, twenty years Rodney's junior, who had three daughters herself from an earlier marriage, all of them grown and married. The letter was overdue, and Rosalyn was already annoyed that he had stayed a month only in London. Headed downstairs an hour later, he saw the morning post in its wire basket on the door behind the letter slot. From the staircase Rodney made out a white envelope within the iron mesh, like a bird lying on the floor of its cage. The image filled him with apprehension. Hesitating on the steps, he thought again of his matutinal messenger.

The letter proved from his London club, details of the annual Derby pool. Another letter lay beneath it, addressed to Morris, his lodger of the previous month. It looked a woman's hand, postmarked Denver, wherever that was. This morning's misgivings aside, Rodney was seldom eager for post. Too often it was merely requests for money, bills of one kind or another. There was a time in his life when three women had looked for money, only one of them to whom he was married. Pocketing the Denver letter, he left the house for the post office on the plaza. Hurrying, he might get Rosalyn's letter out that day.

It was a half-mile through the narrow streets to the plaza, the road rising gently with the hill upon which most of the village sat. The sandstone houses were various shades of umber, leaving the aquamarine and chartreuse shutters to shout aloud their colours. Potted geraniums bloomed by doors, or hung in planters inside the small patios with their piles of firewood. Scattered here and there was the odd *bombona* of bottled gas, itself like an outsized orange flower pot. On Fridays an orange truck with men in orange overalls drove through the village, exchanging a full cylinder for each empty they collected. At first Rodney had difficulty distinguishing shops from ordinary households, as most merchants simply hung a beaded curtain in the doorway to mark their enterprise. Beside the shop he frequented was a pen of black hens with blood-red wattles, too early yet for the old woman in black who often sat among the fowl.

The colours this morning put Rodney again in mind of Morris, who marvelled at the hue and value of everything from soil to sky. Rodney had let the house twice previously, realising enough on the rental to allow himself a hotel holiday elsewhere on the island, a break in his routine. Morris arrived as a lodger, however, and they had shared the house for the month of May. Surprisingly, it came off without a hitch. A painter, the American spent most of his time in the garden, working on studies of nasturtiums, watercolours of the fig and lemon trees. Morris was Bohemian all right, earring and Mexican sandals, but he was an artist after all, whereas the three Dutch every day drinking cognac on the plaza had no such excuse. "Do they live like hippies?" Rodney had asked, upon hearing that Morris had called down to their dwelling.

"No more than we do," the painter had replied, having that afternoon walked through the French doors to find Rodney, jay naked, standing on his head against the garden wall.

In his late-twenties, Morris was quiet for an American, almost taciturn at times. He had been living near Palma with a German holiday guide, until she left him to go back to Berlin. He spoke of any number of women in his life—always with a mournful note, like a bullfrog lonely on a summer night. Indeed his hooded eyes and double chin had Rodney thinking of a frog the evening Morris arrived at the house. After refusing aspirin for a headache that first night, Morris told Rodney that he only used drugs for recreation. The older man laughed, wondering was the painter serious? Not that he especially disapproved, the vice enough of a tradition among the upper classes to open even Kay Wilson's mind. "Whatever was it like?" Kay had quizzed Rosalyn who confessed to once trying her daughter's pot.

"It gave me a better appetite than I've had in years," Rosalyn reported.

Infected by his boarder's enthusiasm for the flora, Rodney had begun to see the garden with fresh eyes. He catalogued his reservations for the American regardless, starting with the date palm that towered above the upstairs veranda. The palm was at the wrong latitude, too far north to bear fruit. The avocado tree, five years in the soil, needed seven to produce. What's more, you could do little with the fruit of the pomegranate, whose best feature was simply its red trumpet-shaped flower. Morris paid scant heed to this grumbling, but perked up when his landlord said the carob tree overhanging the garden wall was possibly the same fruit Odysseus had encountered among the lotus-eaters. Or how the pomegranate was said to have sprung from the spilled blood of Dionysus. His apparent interest was not lost on Rodney, who recalled Gordon's response earlier to these same musings. "I've no time for myth," declared the theosophist, as if Rodney had been on about Black Nationalists or the working class.

Morris had the odd bit of information himself, usually of a vocational nature. Upon learning from Morris of Indian Yellow—a pigment extracted from the urine of cattle foddered on mango leaves—Rodney had replied that Earl Grey tea no longer tasted the same—an observation stemming not so much from any inherent connection as from a singular conversational style, evolved out of years living alone. Not caring overmuch for sequiturs, Rodney often introduced topics from out of the Mediterranean blue. Issuing forth from a prolonged silence at dinner, his conversational sallies had an effect not unlike a gun accidentally discharged.

"Yes, I imagine they were a good excuse to leave home, the Crusades," he would announce, startling Morris who might not always remember a passing reference to the Holy Wars the previous day. Moreover, by leaving home Rodney in fact meant leaving one's wife.

"Speaking of balloons," he would begin when nobody had. "Bicycles have gotten terribly dear," as if Bracken the cat had just pedalled a Raleigh up the garden path.

His manner, which often exasperated Rosalyn, had nearly fifty years in age—plus the breadth of the Atlantic—to its advantage with Morris, who sometimes felt as if he were dining in a BBC costume drama. His host minus a costume perhaps, but fully rigged out in dated opinion, quaint ideas. What's more, there was sport for the two of them in it. "If your house was on fire," Rodney queried, trying to trap the American between his democratic heritage and his vocation, "would you carry out the Rembrandt or your washer woman?"

"Were the choice between your budgerigar and the upstairs maid, would you know yourself?" rejoined the painter, who never failed to point out that Rhodesia was now Zimbabwe, correcting Rodney as a frog might snare an errant fly.

Lamenting the loss of a servant class, the landlord waited on lodger hand and foot, jealous of relinquishing any task that took him through his day. "You've your drawing to do," he pointed out, whenever Morris offered to help with the washing up. If anything, the painter was like a snail in the kitchen, a spoor of colours—pink custard powder or green mint sauce—invariably marking his untidy passage.

When Gordon came to tea one Tuesday, the talk ranged far from the price of butter. Having anticipated a colloquy on the visual arts, Rodney carried the tea-tray out to the garden and into a discussion of hallucinogens. "After reading Huxley's essay," Gordon was expounding, "I very much wanted to try mescaline. For aesthetic purposes, you understand. I thought it would do wonders for my colours!"

"Was it easy to come by?" Rodney asked, passing Morris the scones before he could employ his lodger's reach.

"Not terribly easy, but I did find a doctor in Salisbury who gave me an IQ test. He told me I'd the intelligence to handle it, and agreed to administer a measured dose. He was in poor health, however, and died a fortnight later."

Morris had said little so as not to spoil his fellow painter's story. Before leaving Majorca though, he confided to Rodney how he had taken the drug in question any number of times. "It made the pavement breathe, trees sway," he reported, vaguely disappointing Rodney who recalled claims for marijuana as an aphrodisiac of sorts.

For his part that May afternoon, Rodney had chiefly listened. Conversation with two or more parties proved wearisome after a time. Fading out, Rodney invariably returned through the wrong door.

"London was it?"

"No, Johannesburg," Gordon would reply, leaving Rodney to return to his reverie. Wasn't the impulse to alter consciousness only a natural appetite like sex or hunger, as he had read somewhere? Even as they talked, Bracken lay out cold in the patch of coriander he favoured out of all the garden, the herb long since flattened into a circular bed. No doubt the cat was as high as a kite. Perhaps he would plant catnip for the beast, offer it an alternative to its prevailing dependency. Provided catnip would grow at this latitude, he mused, looking up at the date palm whose sponge-like flowers swarmed with bees. A busy, albeit, fruitless exchange.

Reaching the plaza, Rodney dropped the letters into the *buzon*, trusting the postmaster to forward the Denver envelope with its cancelled postage. A faint breeze stirred the plane trees along the footpath as he overtook two women arm in arm. For no reason he decided to skip lunch: to call on Sally and Roger instead. The walk to their place would do him good.

During his first years in the village, Rodney had walked far and wide. A favourite trek ran west into the mountains, climbing until he reached the monastery set like a stone in the ring of a small hidden valley. Descending, he would order a beer at the small café catering for visitors who drove up Sundays for High Mass in the baroque chapel with its gilded columns. It was years since Rodney had gone to Mass himself. Seated there one afternoon, he remembered wishing—as a child terrified by hell-fire—that he had never been baptised. According to doctrine, he might then face nothing worse than Limbo after death. As he downed his beer, he wondered if his sojourn on Majorca were not that wish prematurely granted? Either way, his life seemed increasingly monk-like these past few years.

He had walked home that night under a full moon, the fields of barley a pale lemon sea broken by the odd solitary tree, moored in the pool of its own black shadow. The round-trip was over thirty kilometres, a distance that impressed the locals no end. Though he still occasionally struck out for the adjoining village on its market day, Rodney no longer walked as much as he had. He should keep at it, he knew. Else he might lose the ability as with anything else. Fears of impotency had proved ungrounded into his seventies, though likely enough you wanted to keep at that also.

As though this were to be a day apart from all habit, Rodney stepped out of himself on the way to Sally's. He hesitated at a hedgehog, flat as a glove beside the road, pausing again to puzzle over a plastic bag full of empty snail shells. The bag had begun to mist over in the sun, tiny drops of condensation like rain on a windscreen. Studying the bag midst the weeds, as though some mystery lay behind its incongruity, he thought of another riddle—engendered more by repetition than ambiguity. One day in January an LP of Tchaikovsky's ballet had arrived from Rosalyn in London. Putting it on the phonograph after dinner, Rodney fell asleep halfway through. That night, pulling his bed out from the bedroom wall which had begun to sweat from the winter rains, he noted for the first time a swan on the mattress label. For several days following then, he was visited by swans. Encountering them on matchboxes from the shop, on packets of sugar with his coffee at the Caves, he puzzled how these items had been without birds of any feather before.

A week later Rodney had visited the local glass factory with the Wilsons, who were showing another niece and her husband the island. Most of the ornaments were of poor quality, the glass thick or streaked with tiny bubbles. Their production, however, was of interest to the visitors, though less of a novelty for the lad in the large shed behind the showroom who made no effort to conceal his boredom. As the party of English looked on, he inserted a long pole into a furnace at the far wall, spinning a lump of molten glass onto its end. Carrying it like a lance to a nearby table, he rolled the glass into a solid disc, rotating the rod along the work surface. Employing clamps and pincers, he drew out a flange on either side, a long thin loop at one end—the wings and neck of a slender swan. Initially fiery orange, the attenuated glass first cooled a sea-green, subsiding to sky-blue. Cutting the swan free of its base, the lad lifted it with tongs into another oven to anneal. "Synchronicity," said Gordon after Rodney described the incidence of incidents, offering him a word, as if a word ever explained anything, for such happenstance.

But the bird at his window signified something, or so insisted Sally when he mentioned it upon reaching their place. Just as a tiny spider betokened a financial windfall, while a larger grey specimen on your sleeve augured a new shirt or jacket. The Irish cook in Wicklow had fed Rodney a similar diet of superstition as a child. A cat or dog into the house with a wisp of straw on its coat foretold of company calling. "There's no end to the things that animals indicate," Sally summed up, only today her heart seemed nowheres in it.

She grew more animated though, telling Rodney of the hen they had recently lost. After it stopped eating for a week, Roger had dosed it with olive oil, thinking it might have sour crop. The bird appeared to improve somewhat, but a neighbour who inspected its mouth declared its tongue was bound. The man removed a tiny flap of skin, and an hour later the hen was dead.

"I decided last night it was time for another round of Spiritual Healing," Sally suddenly changed tack. "I'd felt poorly for days, all aches and pains. Since Roger has the cure, I made him get into bed and hold me the entire night."

"I could feel the sweat pouring off me in rivers," Sally continued, "but I wouldn't let go, and neither did he. By morning I was cured."

"I could feel the sweat running along my ears below the hair line," Roger testified.

"Might you do something for poor Rosalyn's arthritis?" Rodney jested.

"Oh he could, right enough! But she'd have to come down often," added Sally, driving Rodney home with her obtuseness.

Back in time for tea, he discovered there was no bread in the house, the shop shut for siesta. The oversight annoyed him, for Friday evenings, when most of the neighbour women marketed, were hateful, the shop crowded with their noise. He puzzled at their need to shout in such small quarters, apparently a peasant trait once practiced to frighten evil spirits. Gordon held the

Majorcans hollered to show they were in good health, failing to satisfy Rodney who was content to boast of the same in softer tones. He would go for bread as soon as the shop opened, hoping to beat the crowd. Meantime a cup of tea on its own would do no harm.

As he waited on the kettle to boil, Rodney stared at a green smear above the cooker where Morris had killed a fly. His tray of watercolours had attracted them as flame does moths, something sweet-smelling in the pigment. For weeks the house was alive with violet and yellow flies, annoying Rodney only at night when they droned about the sitting room. If he opened a window they would leave, provided there was light enough left to show the way. When Morris remarked it seemed some trouble to take, as opposed to swatting them, Rodney observed it was less than Schweitzer had done in Africa, shifting out of his office until an invasion of ants departed as they had come.

Odd couple that they had made, Rodney missed the artist's company. Their last night together, they had camped on a beach near Alcudia to the north. Driving Rodney's battered Fiat into the scrub pines down along the shore from the resort hotels, they pitched camp on a small bluff overlooking sand and sea. While Morris gathered firewood, Rodney broke out the porcelain butter dish and bread knife from an Edwardian wicker hamper. After tea at the usual hour, the American took an air mattress into the Mediterranean, Rodney a book under the beach umbrella.

Routine gave way to their surroundings at supper time, however, and they were well into a second bottle of wine before the shepherd's pie cleared the fire. After they finished eating, the painter broke out a tiny hash pipe, but septuagenarian Rodney only managed to choke on its smoke.

"Irony is strictly an aristocratic virtue, don't you think?" he asked after he had stopped coughing, his back propped against a pine.

"Virtue?" Morris laughed, hearty with drink and dope.

"In that it demonstrates a detachment from life. You won't find the natives here using irony whatsoever."

"Maybe they've no need for it," Morris said. "Because things turn out pretty much as they expect. Sun-up, sundown, crops failing but once in a blue moon."

"Of course, you artists are romantics at heart," the older man replied, encouraged by the wine. "Though nature—trees and the like—ought to be enough, I suppose, if one is truly self-sufficient ... Or would you eventually go into debt, as it were? Begin to bite your hand which is feeding you?" he trailed off, seemingly encouraged here by hashish as well.

"Do you feel the dope?" Morris queried, peering over the fire.

"Intimacy versus autonomy," the American later suggested when Rodney lamented the close quarters in a marriage bed, the talk having grown sufficiently abstract to lose any peasant. Banking the embers, the two men turned in. An hour later, Rodney rose quietly and shed his clothes. Walking a half-mile down the beach, he had waded into the sea up to his loins, the waves whispering on the sand behind him.

It was on his way home from the shop with the bread that Rodney met the gypsy. A small, dark, clever man, the gypsy lived on the other side of the village with a timid, cross-eyed wife and several children. Once or twice a year he offered to sell

Rodney something: an old motorbike, a young dog, a cheap radio. This evening he merely wanted to talk.

"*A donde vas*?" the gypsy grinned. "Where are you going?"

"I'm not going anywhere," Rodney blurted, unnerved as always by this dark-skinned man who reminded him of the peons on the Brazilian farm. When he was bold as a child, the cook in Wicklow would threaten him with the tinkers who camped by the river in their horse-drawn carts.

"Always walking?" the gypsy observed, smiling beneath his soft-brimmed cap.

"*Caminando es la mitad de la salud*," said Rodney without thinking. "Walking is half your health." He felt absurd, nevertheless pleased at having more or less translated a favourite axiom.

"*Salud, dinero y amor!*" the gypsy beamed his delight. "Health, money and love," he repeated, proffering the words like coins on his outstretched palm.

"Yes, and you, are you well?" Rodney lunged, endeavouring to get the exchange back onto conventional ground—where he could take leave of it.

Shrugging, the gypsy took Rodney's query literally. Pulling his shirt from his trousers, he revealed a bandage neatly wound about his lower abdomen, the white fabric almost lustrous against the dark skin. A stranger to all convention, the gypsy took Rodney's hand, pressing it against his bare torso above the dressing. The first flesh the old man had touched in months, it felt hot to his fingers, surprisingly alive.

Later, well past his bedtime, Rodney sat on in the garden. Sat on in a night painted by Rousseau, the moon behind the fronds of the date palm, its light on the tiny leaves of a mandarin tree. Bracken, if not entirely tiger-like, lay nonetheless regarding Rodney through a clump of iris. As he listened to the breeze in the orchard, Rodney heard the repetitive cry of some bird that broke into a double-note the farther away it sounded. For years he had puzzled over the nightjar which he had never heard, trying to imagine a birdcall that might live up to its name. Disappointed by asphodel, and by the Northern Lights when he ultimately encountered them, Rodney suspected the nightjar would only let him down as well. Honeymooning with his second wife, he had run through the streets of Florence to see Michelangelo's 'David', arriving just as the gallery doors closed to the public. Their train had departed shortly after, leaving Rodney with a more vivid memory of that futile effort than any actual sculpture had ever imparted—as if what you fail to experience is what remains truly poignant.

Or what takes you by surprise, like the Graf Zeppelin suddenly filling the upstairs window of a Rio brothel, blotting out the sky. Or the surprising warmth of the gypsy's flesh beneath his hand. Unsettled by that encounter, Rodney had returned to the house where he decided to forego dinner for a sandwich. As he cut the fresh loaf, he thought of the eponymous Earl, then of Lord Cardigan who similarly handed down his name, wondering had they fathered children besides? Slicing some cheese, he remembered reading somewhere that infidelity was rare among gypsies, who married at fourteen never to leave their wives.

Leaving the kitchen, he had gone into the garden to wait out the turmoil within. *Salud, dinero y amor*, he would inform his circle, all of them birds of a feather: theosophists open to every mystery but love, expatriates and artists whose worlds of colour looked no less lonely than his own, however much peopled with cat and dog. Whatever their powers, the carpenter and clairvoyant at least had each other, albeit soaked in sweat.

Three days later Rodney found a small bird on the dusty road beneath his bedroom window. There was no mark on its body, and he suspected Bracken too well-fed to hunt. In Brazil, bats lying along the road suggested an incidence of rabies. Whether in Wicklow a fallen sparrow betokened something else, here on Majorca it need not signify. No longer out of phase, he would no longer trouble himself over import and design, accepting with habitual equanimity the fact that he had again dreamt of swans over successive nights. Gently shifting the bird with his foot into a patch of wild fennel, he turned toward the house, thinking it nearly time for lunch.

OPEN SEASON

FIRST THOUGHTS upon waking were of the warren, sufficient to turn Graham out of bed. Seldom rising before Sara, he took care these mornings not to disturb her. In the dim light he noted how quietly she slept, features veiled by her wayward hair. If the bedclothes were awry, he replaced them, touching her gently, the caress without tension only for her being asleep. Sara was unhappy with her upper arms, too heavy she thought, though in fact she was entirely slender. Oddly enough, the limbs she disliked were often cold to his touch, the rest of her sleeping self bed-warm.

The morning was again mild and grey, mist down over the mountain opposite. It was early to be up and about for November, a full hour before the neighbouring cottages would show any smoke. If not the archetypal hunter at dawn, Graham nonetheless felt especially alive, happy to be in motion at this hour. Upon leaving the cottage he took his usual route: a mile of road that brought him to the warren behind the dunes that backed the large strand. Skirting the gate secured with bailing twine, he stepped over the wire fence itself, holding it down between his legs. Before him several potato pits thatched with grass looked like burial mounds. Beyond them, he counted at least seven rabbits running for cover. The warren was living with them, but over a fortnight he had failed to take a single one.

This morning was no exception. Four snares lay undisturbed at the entrance to various burrows, a fifth knocked askew. At the last of the six snares set, the wire loop was gone: the holding cord severed, its stake loosened, tufts of fur scattered about like bog cotton. Moving quickly, Graham reset the fifth snare, then headed home.

At home, he found Sara already at work in the upper room that served as her studio. "There's porridge on the cooker," she told him. She did not ask about the warren, and Graham did not volunteer. Sara was often temperamental mornings, a small lump of testiness she soon shifted, like clearing her throat. Only lately her ill humour seemed to last the entire day, colouring the recent unease between them. In turn Graham had grown tentative, cautious, resentful. When love goes wrong, it alters both lovers along with the terrain, making it difficult to gauge the exact degree of change. In many ways Sara was still her same optimistic, sunny self—if the milk soured, it would do for baking bread—only she no longer shone on Graham.

At first Graham assumed they would see it out, that things would come round, himself by nature rarely inclined to dig in and confront. At best they had tip-toed once or twice around the tension, acknowledging their close quarters in the tiny cottage, their isolation on the west coast of Ireland, the long winter nights setting in. Having already survived these conditions for three years, however, both of them knew it was something more.

Graham and Sara had first come to Carrigan on holiday. Then, after falling for the tiny village by the sea, the sparsely settled glen backed by empty mountains overlooking bogland barren as the moon, they had returned to England and sold everything. Five years married, they decided to trade their terraced house in a Cotswolds town, flower garden and fishpool, for a windswept stretch of Irish coast that somehow seemed to promise more. If artists and artisans were everywhere in England, there also existed a network of guilds and craft-fairs, opportunities for nixers and part-time work. To move to Carrigan was to gamble on selling enough of their wares to feed themselves.

So far they had managed, Graham building a small shop at the front of his pottery, and Sara finding a Dublin gallery to show her drawings and tapestries. Unlike the South African silversmiths who had since left Carrigan, Graham and Sara had no children, a circumstance which no doubt favoured their undertaking. English in Ireland, they were neither native nor visitor, neither fowl nor fish. If they had not yet made close friends in the village, they had adapted well, adopting the seasonal routines of bog and garden that helped to fill the hours, days even, that simply do not exist in an English town. Loneliness was considerable, but they had one another. Old friends came to stay for a week at a time. For three years it had seemed a proper life.

Then this autumn they had lost each other. There came no single incident to mark the event, nothing like the first night of hard frost that takes out mustard and cress in a single breath. Rather they had simply drifted apart—inevitably perhaps, given the wide expanse of sea and moor surrounding them. Drifting, yet tethered—like two boats lost at sea—they mostly narked and bitched at one another, disputing matters of no consequence. Something precious was being squandered, yet they contented themselves by totting up the pin money.

Like many marriages, theirs too had woven itself around the unavoidable strands of contention. In their case, however, both of them were more inclined to meet such incidence with humour than with anger. In time, repeated incidents became domestic jokes. Unable ever to agree if the moon were full, they differed on principle, laughing up at the night sky. "You can't lead and follow both," Sara chided another evening shortly after they had moved to Carrigan, taking the torch from Graham as they picked their way up the hill above the cottage. A fleet of trawlers out after herring had appeared on the horizon, and they decided to climb the hill in the dark for a better look at the string of lights, like a row of street-lamps out to sea. That you can't lead and follow both had become a domestic aphorism from that evening on. Yet while they had always sparred, there now seemed less room for disputation. Only the previous day an argument over a bird briefly glimpsed in the meadow below—whether magpie or carrion crow—had ended in bitterness. Such behaviour was absurd, but there seemed no way out.

So they retreated: Sara into her studio, Graham to his pottery in a converted byre beside the cottage. November was a slow time of year, however, the pottery a cold place besides. As a rule Graham threw few pots through the winter, as he was able to turn out most of what sold during spring and summer, when the village saw a steady, if thin, stream of tourists. Most of the visitors were Irish, some English, a growing number of Germans, a scattering of French. And so this November

Graham had discovered the warren, the pursuit of rabbits coming almost as a godsend.

The hunt was a joint venture with Watty, who had sold Graham and Sara the cottage, having built himself a new bungalow nearby. A subsistence farmer like most in the village, he put in potatoes on a patch of meadow adjoining the warren. The sandy soil there was considered beneficial for Banners, and it was not far from this field that he and Graham set their snares.

"If you were digging spuds, they'd be in at your heels," Watty muttered the third or fourth time they found the snares undisturbed. However November was a slow season for Watty also, and hunting rabbits was diversion enough. Seldom ever at their cottage, Watty now called in most afternoons. Seated by the range the older man whittled on scraps of pine. Seated across, Graham appreciated the economy of movement, the single turn of his knife that notched each stake at the top where the holding cord was affixed. His admiration was not unlike that of summer visitors who watched the potter himself at work on his wheel. While they invariably asked the same questions—did he dig his own clay and so on— he and Watty talked little enough. The holding cords Watty fashioned from nylon yarn. Forty winters on the hand loom inside his cottage, Watty managed thread like a magician. Anchoring one end with his boot, he would twist a length of yarn, bringing the other end down to the floor. Both ends secured by his boot, the yarn would spin itself into a double strand.

"One time you could buy snares in the shop," Watty explained. "With a nice brass eye, same as you have in a shoe."

His presence did little to ease the household, for he and Sara did not get on.

"He's too cute by half," Sara informed Graham their very first spring, after asking Watty had he any muck they could spread on the garden.

"Muck? What kind of a flower is that?" the neighbour jested.

Sara had not laughed in turn. Tall, pale and slender, with long red hair, she probably looked herself like some tropical flower to Watty, lovely but utterly exotic. Pleased at knowing to call it muck, not manure, Sara felt the farmer had not played fair, refusing his own idiom like some foreign currency. Even now Watty attempted the odd joke with her, but Sara usually left the kitchen to them, Graham to tidy up the wood shavings after Watty departed.

In actuality the two men spent more time along the road, in conversation with villagers whom Graham scarcely knew, than they did upon the warren. Most of these locals were sixty or more; single or married men, they all lived like bachelors. Days were spent on chores out of doors, weather permitting. Evenings in the pub where a local woman rarely ventured. Leaning against a stone ditch, Graham listened more than he spoke, the talk as much a ritual as the hunt itself, with its own fascination.

"Many's the rabbit I ate."

"They're good eating this time of year."

"You only find rabbits on kindly ground."

Every man was an authority, and they no more agreed on how to trap game than they did on winning turf or saving hay.

Indeed Sara insisted most of them went to the bog chiefly to keep a critical eye on how their neighbour mismanaged the task to hand. Unlike the English couple, however, the villagers thrived on disputation, considerations of varying technique.

Peadar, one of two bachelors in a two-storey house above the warren, held it was four fingers high, not three, the wire loop should hang above the ground. "You can always prop it with a wee slip of grass," he allowed. His brother James recalled their father hunting with a ferret, killing twenty rabbits in a day. The only hitch was the ferret might kill the rabbit below, feed and fall asleep, yourself waiting in attendance above. One solution was to break the ferret's teeth.

"You'd want to do that," Peadar agreed. "Else the ferret could cut your throat as you slept, were it to get loose in the house."

"A hump at the shoulder," James observed. "Not a bone in their body, they can twist every which way." For Graham "to ferret out" would hold an immediacy ever after, the phrase made flesh by these old men above the road.

"Hold it by the hind legs," Watty instructed when Graham asked how they would dispose of a rabbit still alive in the snare. "Then clip it behind the ears with the heel of your palm," his hand describing the rabbit punch which Graham had never before linked with the act itself. To the potter, such literalness seemed one of the benefits of country life, where the cock atop the dung heap was a familiar sight.

"A rabbit is hard to get," Watty excused their luck after a week.

"The rabbit is fit to fool you," conceded Peadar. Despite the severed cords, Peadar maintained the rabbit never bit through anything. "It struggles until the cord gives way, else it dies."

His brother however contended the rabbit chewed the cord. "Horsehair works well," James explained. "Three or four strands plaited together are too slippery for the teeth to get a purchase."

"Horsehair works well—when there were horses!" Peadar said, implying a rabbit chewed only grass.

For his part Graham wondered was someone stealing from the snares? Using a knife to cut the cord? Plausible or not, he held back from broaching a possibility the others had skirted. The likelihood was only indirectly addressed, the morning James told of Petey Gara who had lived in a farflung townland years before. "Whatever ability he had, let you lift from his snares, hare or bird, and he'd know it was you who'd done the job. The next morning Petey would be at your door, making inquiries."

Lacking for company, Graham and Sara generally shared all chance encounters, parcelling out any chat in the shop for whoever had stayed home. His outings to the warren, however, Graham kept to himself, his selfishness in response to her withdrawal. Certainly his reticence was not to spare Sara any coarseness; however Sara appeared to Watty, she was no hothouse orchid. While neither of them ate much meat, Sara readily cleaned what fish Graham killed at the rocks below, bloodying her hands without a thought. And once, when she did object to a tale, her response was not unreasonable.

Peadar and James had been on about rats that day, debating the merits of several poisons sold in the shop. With one brand the rat swelled up. Stricken by the other, it withered. "Ach, it's much of a muchness," interjected Watty, "provided the rat goes out of the house to die." He went on then to tell of his uncle who had carried a bundle of thatch up a ladder onto a roof. Undoing the straw, the uncle felt something run up his trouser leg.

"He seizes a lump along his thigh," Graham recounted at home, "and tears the bit away, cloth and rat both ..."

"I don't care to hear anymore," Sara said.

Increasingly drawn into such company, Graham spoke little of this fraternity. Passive, almost paralyzed in the cottage, he welcomed the simple activity of the hunt, the requisite cunning he was unable to turn to a faltering marriage. Still it was in many ways an alien world, and Graham proceeded slowly. For three years he had been content merely to shout aloud as he passed the warren, delighted to startle the rabbits whose dark forms bounded across the open space. Though he had fished since childhood, he had always considered hunting as somehow out of bounds. Certainly his pottery hinted at a more whimsical self, candlesticks and reliquaries adorned with wee beasts and birds. Seemingly it was an open season for change all around.

Graham continued to rise early for another week. Late summer had seen pools of yellow ragwort, golden stooks of oats and rye beside the warren. Now the colours were duller, the grass eaten to the ground, like a worn carpet underfoot. Hoping to set new snares, he tried to establish into which holes the rabbits ran. Yet all too often they disappeared behind a rise or a lump of rushes, leaving him a choice of burrows. Their vanishing act reminded Graham of how from the road he sometimes lost sight of a figure walking through the dunes beyond the warren, something elusive in the very lay of the land. Standing in the centre of the warren, he saw how Carrigan itself disappeared, as if the village were set in a cup or bowl, rimmed by mountains and sea.

That weekend he and Sara fought over the fire grown cold in Graham's absence.

"I thought there were enough embers when I got up."

"You might have thrown on more turf regardless," Sara said. "A pity you care more about those rabbits," she pursued as if determined to draw his ire, "than you do the sheep."

"Damn the bloody sheep," Graham flared. "To hell with it all!" he said, hurling his tea mug at the wall beside the range. Arguably a potter's privilege, though any crockery he had heretofore thrown was always on the pottery wheel. And yet it mattered not, as Sara had simply departed the kitchen.

The sheep in question Graham fashioned in fleecy repose, tiny horns, faces painted black like Watty's sheep on the hill. "Scottish Highland breed," he would mutter on summer days, hustling the odd visitor from Paisley or Edinburgh. A popular item, the sheep were tedious to turn out in lots of fifty, and he resented Sara fretting over them in November, even if they were the task to hand.

The momentary release occasioned by the shattered delft reminded Graham of their lovemaking the previous night. A reprieve of the body only, bringing them no closer, once they were no longer enjoined. Turning on the pottery radio, he heard the end of a traditional fiddle tune. "Woman of the House, What Ails Ye?" announced the presenter, making Graham only hope that Sara too had the radio on.

It was that same afternoon that the dogs first turned up outside the cottage, to reappear at odd hours over the next three days, always a pair of them in it. The larger grey dog staked his claim to the grassy bank above the garden, periodically rising onto his haunches to howl. A younger black-and-white border collie whined outside the pottery door. Were Watty's bitch in heat, she was nowhere in evidence. Absurd as it was, Graham could not help feeling the creatures sensed a deterioration within, something rank about the household.

Reluctant to drive them off, he likewise refrained from inquiring of Watty an explanation. All too likely there was some folklore involved: if you shot a hare, there were white hairs in its tail you needed to pluck for luck before bringing it indoors. And, while he did not give in to such fancy, Graham did not on this occasion care to hear of it either. Earlier that week Peadar had told of a villager who once brought a hare into the house. Sharp words had ensued, and the man had flung the game at his wife to be dressed. The woman was with child, and three months later gave birth to a boy with a wrinkled upper lip.

When on the fourth day the dogs failed to return, Graham sensed Sara was equally relieved, their life already too much the poor parody of some Bergman film, a claustrophobic study of domestic tension against a backdrop of wind and rain. Then, a week later, Sara left. When she rose early that Monday, Graham assumed it was to begin another day, hardly to catch the eight o'clock bus from the village. No longer rising for the rabbits, he got up an hour after to find a note on the kitchen table. She was for Dublin, then England, a few lines about the need for a change. Time for herself, some space as well. Graham laughed upon reading that—as though more time and space existed than was on offer in Carrigan. Sufficient, at least, to have set them spinning apart, in opposite fashion to the thread secured beneath Watty's boot.

There would be ample opportunity, Graham knew, to look within. At the moment, however, the easiest answers came from the lay of the land. "I miss the trees, Graham," Sara had remarked only the day before, suggesting the two of them had perhaps run out of kindly ground. Or that only a dullard could live at the sea's edge without learning something of the nature of change. Acknowledging an initial relief, he knew the pain of her leaving lurked behind hedgerows farther down the road. Meantime he marvelled at a sudden stab of anxiety over who would now cut his hair?

Once up, he took care to feed the range before making himself a cup of tea. He did the washing up next, honouring the usual routine, as if the tried-and-not-so-true were struggling to maintain its sway. Opening the pottery door, he heard the panicked flight of the bird straight off. Every few months a starling worked its way within under the eaves. Once he had found a fledgling, its neck broken, lying beneath the large window that looked onto the sea. Outside, the sun had brought to life the red-and-green highlights along its wings. Moving slowly to avoid frightening it further, Graham opened the window, standing behind the kiln until the bird escaped. Taking a rag, he wiped up the bird shit scattered everywhere, like tiny random spatters of glaze.

He had two-dozen sheep ready for firing when Watty called in. Seated, the farmer began to reminisce about the byre that had preceded the pottery. "Many's the animal I lost in here," Watty pointed his pipe at the corner where a blue heifer had failed. Two cows had died the following year along the west wall. Another December his donkey walked out the door and dropped. Listening to Watty catalogue his losses, Graham suddenly wondered whether the place was cursed.

"How's the Missus?" Watty inquired next.

"No change, but comfortable," Graham wanted to reply, as if Sara were in her sickbed.

"She's gone to Dublin for a few days," he answered instead, wondering had Sara been seen, case in hand, along the road? While conversation with the locals often resembled a game of draughts, it was the chess-match of his own marriage that had seemingly stalemated itself this morning.

"Nothing doing on the warren?" Watty asked.

"I found two snares cut again last evening," Graham said. This time, honouring his impulse, he asked the older man straight out, "Is someone stealing from the snares?"

"You wouldn't know," Watty deferred, again mentioning Petey Gara who had always known. Only now Watty made it sound not so much theft as the done thing—to lift from any snare you stumbled across. Loading his pipe like a musket, the older man went out to weave.

That afternoon Graham went down to the strand, forsaking the sheep who had multiplied to a flock of forty. The wind had come round to the north, its slight sting hinting at the imminent winter—like an outsized cat crouched the far side of the mountain, claws unsheathed. Clots of wrack lay along the sand, a few bits of driftwood, and a scattering of spent shotgun shells, their bright oranges and reds at odd intervals like a recurring thought. How often Sara and he had walked the strand, foraging for the fire, stripping seaweed from the rocks at low tide in March to mulch the garden. Braced against the inevitable hurt, he found such memory curiously deflated, like beer gone flat, watercolours whose hues have faded. He guessed the suddenness of Sara's departure had provided its own anaesthetic, the shock that numbs the sudden blow. Her note upon the kitchen table a cliché as worthy of film or fiction as was this splendid setting of mountain and sea. And hadn't they first met in similar story-book fashion? At midnight in the middle of a frozen English lake during a Christmas holiday. "It's unlucky to meet a red-haired woman at the outset of a journey," Watty once informed them, the superstition amusing Graham as much as it had nettled Sara.

The next morning the post brought them each a letter. The envelope from Sara's Dublin gallery boasted a new stamp. Part of a wildlife series; *lepus timidus hibernicus*, a large Irish hare. Graham looked at it with especial interest, noting the powerful hind legs and outsized ears. Inside was a brief note on a tapestry exhibition in the spring, signed simply Thomas. Of a sudden Graham wondered had Sara taken a lover among that crowd, the three or four trips she had taken alone to Dublin over the past year? If so, he hadn't the powers of a Petey Gara, not a clue as to where he might head to claim her back.

The other letter was from a Scottish friend, a leather worker with a small studio near the Mull of Kintyre. Peadar, who had worked over there, told how years ago Scottish farmers would bring in rabbits from other shires to offset sub-breeding. Going out every autumn with ferrets and guns, killing enough rabbits in a single day to pay their annual rent. 'You and Sara should think of coming over at Christmas,' the letter concluded.

Stepping out of the cottage, Graham found the north wind had torn the cloud cover overhead, wide swathes of sunlight now illuminating the distant hills. Five or six starlings sat on the telephone line above the road, their oily feathers blown ragged by the wind that sang in the wire. Above the meadow opposite, a lump of rooks darted and swooped—their flight pattern like iron filings bewitched by a hidden magnet. Whether he holidayed in Scotland or not, Graham sensed in the very splendour before him that he was not much longer for the West of Ireland. Here was very much a country for old men— to misquote the poet. Bereft of a lover's arms, you risked being seduced by a beguiling severity of sea and sky.

"It's not every man can get a woman," James had once joked, only to be interrupted by Peadar who informed Graham that a rabbit freshly killed on the road made fine eating. "Provided it's only clipped on the head, not crushed."

"Only the odd hare, but no rabbit," Watty had quipped on another occasion, sounding like a sexual reference, though Graham heard next to nothing from his companions of what was locally dubbed 'bad chat'. Rather it was an unadulterated kind of masculine company they offered, quite simply a world of men without women.

That night Graham hunted up the hot water jar, having wakened with a chill. "The bed's too cold without you," he sang to himself, misquoting the song, waiting on the kettle. Lifting it from the range, he thought again about clearing off, wondering would he even last until Christmas? Small wonder he might shrink from his future prospects in Carrigan: a steady diet of road kills together with wintery sheets. Slipping the water jar beneath the blankets, Graham saw a long red hair upon the pillow, like the thinnest strand of copper wire. Stopped short by the metaphor, he puzzled over just what exactly he had been trying to trap this season, as if love could be ensnared in such simple fashion.

"Hare today, gone tomorrow," he offered aloud—as if tiring of his own lyricism, no longer able for a storybook style. Looking out their bedroom window, he saw the moon balanced like a newly minted copper on the headland across the bay. Her orb looked to be full, and he had nobody at his side to dispute it.

THE DRAUGHTSMAN AND
THE UNICORN

ONCE UPON A TIME has its merits—even for a story where twice and thrice is perhaps closer to the truth. Or should I say closer to the mark, for those who insist upon distinguishing between fact and the fabulous? Either way, the time—this time around—was August of last year, the kind of summer that occasionally graces Ireland. The sun makes its entrance in early spring, returning daily until it promises to split the very stones. By midsummer its rule is so absolute you forget the melancholy, the mist and damp that generally reign.

Thus last August was glorious in Glenmore, an ideal season for visitors. Scant risk of falling out with friends, cabin-bound by the rain, as often happens here when company calls. What's more, my harvest guest was Nicolas, with whom I could happily pass a fortnight in a hatbox. Lively, affable, well-able to look after himself, Nicolas is of *luftmensch* lineage, as my grandmother would say. 'Men of air' who operate without timetables, floating through life in irresponsible, solipsistic fashion.

My dismaying grandmother believes I'm also of that tribe, but the charges better fit Nick, who has never settled anywhere as I have in Glenmore these past three years. Aix-en-Provence is as much of a nest as Nicolas has, stopping there with a French woman and their child for months at a time. The rest of the year he roams: making music by the Aegean or chalk drawings in Lapland, wherever one finds footpaths there.

In July a postcard arrives. Nick is due shortly in Ireland with a hang-glider, intending to throw himself off the Dingle Peninsula and the Cliffs of Moher, plus whatever heights the parish of Glenmore might afford. I hear nothing further, until the mutter of a faulty exhaust one August afternoon. Outside my cottage I find a battered van, Nick at the wheel. On its roof secured with line lies his other vehicle: a trussed-up bird of blue and green silk.

What's more, Nicolas has—following his London patois— another bird along. A German lass, scarcely five-foot tall, blue overalls holed at the knee. Atop her cropped blond head sits a kind of cone, a few strands of red yarn affixed to its apex, secured by a similar thread under her chin. "Timothy, painter, meet Elke, unicorn," Nick says as we shake hands. Trying not to stare at her headgear, I see straight off what can only be described as true-blue eyes.

We stand for a moment, taking in the view from my garden. Below the road, a meadow slopes two hundred yards to the sea. A mile across the bay is a massive promontory, a watchtower at its extremity. All of what we espy lies bathed in the late-afternoon light. "That looks likely," Nicolas says at last, indicating the headland which rises seven-hundred feet above the sea.

"You must be mad!" I opine. In fact the highest sea-cliff in Europe lies just south, and I'm relieved Nick has set his sights to the north. As he rummages in his van, I peer over his shoulder. Midst the jumble lie his guitar, a box of coffee filters, a carton of foodstuffs, an oil lamp. The interior of the van is covered in fabric, batiked blue with cottony clouds along the roof. Below the windows runs a clothesline, pegged with singlets and socks.

Elke takes her tea in silence, departs to walk the large strand towards the village. As Nick tops up my mug, I bring out a few pastels, knowing he draws only in chalk. "Have you paintings?" he asks, but I defer, reluctant to show them just yet. Taking out a tin emblazoned *Travel Sweets*, he rolls us both a cigarette. "We'd a row before I left," Nick says when I ask after his father, a London architect. "He wanted me to take on another project, but I declined." Trained as a draughtsman, Nicolas occasionally freelances with his father's firm. "I'd just finished a job for him, which paid for the glider. I thought he'd be pleased at my acquiring some chattel," Nick adds, "but when he heard how I'd spent my pay packet, he went quite mad!"

"It's portable property, that and the van," I point out, "and as such they don't qualify. Still, you want to travel light," reminding him of what he has so often reminded me.

"I've a buyer for both lined up in France," Nick grins as if to reassure me.

"What luck had you in Kerry and Clare?"

"Soaring inland was spot-on, but I couldn't fly near the sea at all. All this sun on the water makes the wind mad along the cliffs."

"Did you get to Dingle," I ask. A locale not unlike Glenmore, only marginally warmer winters.

"That's where I met Elke."

"Oh, did you now?" I bait him. I fail to get a rise however, Nick at thirty-two already a wise old trout. I remember reading somewhere how gypsies seldom sleep around, and thinking straight off of Nick, who sleeps alone everywhere but Aix-en-Provence.

"I was walking Slea Head when I came on Elke. She was seated at the very edge, leaning so far forward I didn't dare hail her. Instead, I managed to angle into her peripheral vision."

"What was up?"

"She'd lost a boot below, and was weighing whether to follow suit."

"Leap into the abyss?"

"Something like that."

"All for a boot?"

"A white wellington, mind you, not just any boot."

"Unicorn?" I query at last.

"With white hooves no less," Nick nods approvingly, a teacher with time for even the obtuse among his charges.

"I don't understand."

"Who spoke of that?"

Nonetheless Elke had retreated from the edge. In a Dingle pub she told Nick of seeing *The Last Unicorn*, staged at Edinburgh a month before. After the performance, Elke cut her hair and painted her boots. Jettisoning her pink bicycle, she struck out on foot for the ferry to Ireland.

"Her horn?" I ask Nick.

"A bobbin for yarn, a gift from a Highlands weaver."

"You look in her eyes, they're blue and nobody's home?" I borrow from that summer's hottest single.

"Oh, she's at home," Nick counters, "she just wanders off now and again."

Elke wandered no farther than the strand that afternoon, returning to help with supper. Too tired for the pub, my guests retire shortly after. I give Nick the loft in the upper room, clear the cluttered couch for myself in the lower room which serves me as studio. Elke draws the settle bed in the kitchen where I sleep in winter. At supper I had noticed how alike she and Nicolas were, fair-haired and finely featured, siblings as Botticelli might have sketched them.

The next morning we walk up to the tower across the bay. Dating from the Napoleonic Wars, it was built with local stone fixed by mortar made from quicklime and oxen-blood. Several such towers still stand along this coast, interiors gutted, windows open to the wind. At the summit we try not to startle a few sheep grazing beyond the tower. Years back the villagers kept goats on these cliffs. To keep the less-agile sheep, which are loath to feed where they scent goat, back from the edge.

"Are there goats left?" Elke asks with a sobriety befitting one who fancies herself the last of her kind.

"It suits you," I want to say today of her horn—only it seems rather like commenting on her nose or chin.

"Seemingly a half-dozen or so, all wild," I remark instead. "But I've never seen a one."

Lying on our bellies at the edge, we watch a small hawk below us chase a trio of rooks who likely roost in the tower.

Cloud shadows lie on the surface of the sea, like so many patches of wrack below the water, the wash against the rocks like a border of lace. Below, a pair of gulls ride the air-stream up the banks, soaring ever skyward. Tailing off and down toward the sea, they again approach the cliff, shooting up over our heads again.

"They're doing what I'll attempt tomorrow," Nicolas declares. Elke and I say nothing. No doubt her mind is elsewhere, and mad as Nick's flight plan sounds, I find the responsibility for myself an outsized task at the best of times.

"With luck, you can circle in an eddy for hours," he adds. Lying on, we listen as Nick explains the powerful updraught at the edge of a sea cliff, engendered by the wind silk-smooth off the water.

That afternoon Elke and I go down to the sea, leaving Nick to write to his father. Crossing the meadow, we pass a Friesian cow heavy with calf. Elke en route gathers a bouquet of sea-pinks, losing them as we scramble down rocks to the water. While I harvest mussels, she picks her way among tidal pools on the barnacled ledge. This afternoon she looks a kind of sprite in motley, wearing a patchwork sweater against the breeze, horn bobbing as she leaps from rock to rock.

When I have enough shellfish, we sit together at the water's edge. Her jumper I see now is a compilation of knitted remnants: one sleeve cashmere, the other Aran knit, the torso of Peruvian alpaca, three or four feathers worked into the weave across her breast. On her horn are drawn tiny stars and a moon, the detail already faded from the summer sun.

"My mother leaves me always in my pram," Elke says when I remark the feathers. "So I amuse myself by picking at my pillow. By the time she remembers me, I am covered in feathers from foot to head."

Heading home, Elke points out another cow—what might look a hefty Hereford halfway up the meadow. I laugh, saying nothing. Approaching, Elke finds her bovine is but a rusted oil drum, filling a gap in the low stone ditch. "How, now, brown cow?" I jest, but Elke insists on what she saw. In the cottage I make her and Nick a cup of tea, before hunting down a passage in Emerson, who wonders whether fish or oxen in the meadow are immutably fish or oxen, or only so appear? I can't gauge if the nineteenth-century prose in a foreign tongue is too much for her or not. Nodding, she asks have I a hair brush, as she undoes her horn.

Steaming the mussels, I sauté them in garlic and butter, fix a salad of radish and greens. Taking our meal into the garden, we watch the evening light upon the sea and headland. When I suggest the pub, Elke assents, but Nick prefers to stay in and play his guitar. If he seems dispirited, I lay it to the falling out with his father. Distracted by his elfin companion, I plan to sit down with him tomorrow.

In the pub Roddy draws two pints with customary aplomb, like those in legend who are unable to see a unicorn. Nor do the other villagers bat an eye at Elke's get-up, having seen every class of tramp and blow-in before, from one-eyed dogs to Scandinavian blondes. The place is full of summer visitors, but we find a table in a corner. In winter, with three or four locals only, the pub is a different place, more like a medieval tavern. Even now as I watch, a villager by the door slowly takes a pipe-stem from a pocket, twisting it easily into its bowl. Something in that deliberate economy of motion, his huge bulk in a tattered jacket, evokes an ancient peasantry. At times other such scenes surface out of Brueghel: a fisherman silhouetted with an outsized pole against the sky, an authenticity of image little short of mythic in the fading light.

After a while Elke says she has a game for us. Taking a tissue from her overalls, she draws it tightly over my empty glass, securing it with an elastic. Centring a coin on it, she explains we are to torch the tissue with a cigarette in turn. Whoever causes the penny to drop into the glass buys another round.

As Elke applies her smoldering *Gitane* to the tissue, a tiny circle of fire widens slightly, then winks out. I lack her touch, and burn a large hole at the edge. Sharing the cigarette, we transform the tissue into a sea of islands and inlets edged in black, the penny suspended in a delicate hammock of lace. Again at the edge, I barely scorch the tissue. Hesitating, I try again. This time however the ember severs an isthmus, drops the penny into the drink as Elke claps in delight.

"Did I need to try twice?" I ask, rising to buy another round.

"That's up to you," my gypsy pal replies, handing me the day's lesson. Indeed it is entirely up to me—which explains the siblings' kiss we exchange upon saying goodnight. Anything more is up to me, and I sense myself no match for this unicorn. "You live like a monk here," she has told me earlier, as if challenging me to prove otherwise. Outstripped by her impulsiveness, I am also apprehensive—as if Elke were best approached obliquely, cautiously, much in the way Nicolas angled in high above the sea on Dingle.

Nick is first up in the morning, off in the van before I rise. A sea breeze is softest before the sun warms the water, and such a mild wind is best for a launch. I had offered to accompany him, but Nick prefers to go it alone. A dirt track runs part of the way to the tower, leaving him a half-mile of bog over which to carry his craft.

After breakfast Elke departs to forage for magic mushrooms—more ways of flying than wings alone. It's early in the season for them, but I mention a few likely spots, advising her to look out for signs of sheep.

"Sheeps eat them?"

"How else," I laugh, "do they graze up and down the cliffs?"

Alone again, I retire to my studio. Since spring I have been painting hats. First in a series of still-lives was an old tweed cap found in a drawer. On paper it became a vaguely ominous bivalve: an outsized oyster, the metal snap on its brim gleaming like a pearl. Next I selected a black beret I've worn for years. Endowed with fringe and a purple wash, it emerged as a kind of mussel, a tassel of seaweed at either end. More recently I have struggled with a woman's fancy hat, purchased at an antique shop in a nearby town. Made of mauve felt with a scalloped brim, it boasts a feathered wing on either side. On paper, however, I've only come up with some species of strange bird, faintly sinister in its huddled repose.

This morning I jot down notes for a drawing of cows, an idea seeded by both Elke and Emerson. As I write, I notice on the table how a Chinese watercolour brush, fashioned of sheep's wool, suddenly suggests a fishing fly favoured in

Glenmore for catching mackerel. Metamorphosis seems the order of the day.

After lunch I head out, seduced once again by the lovely weather, as has happened all summer. Indoors I had imagined Nicolas circling like a multi-hued hawk across the bay, but once outdoors I see only his van halfway up the headland. Tempted to hike his way, I choose instead the large strand. Following its estuary into the village, I stop at the pub for a beer. Five minutes later, amid great excitement, Nicolas is carried in.

Three men set him gently on the padded bench along the window. Conscious, presumably in great pain, he manages a wink all the same. As Roddy brings over a tumbler of brandy, his wife rings the village doctor. For a time Nick says nothing, sips the brandy. His right arm and left leg don't look right, but he has, against considerable odds, survived. Within minutes the pub fills up, villagers, visitors, and Elke who joins me by his side.

Slowly Nick tells how the turbulence upon his launch takes him by surprise, throwing him into a stall. Unable to mount the updraught, he is forced to dive deliberately seawards in an attempt to regain air-speed. Fifty yards down, however, a vicious vortex of wind spins him into the cliff, snapping a cable. Out of control, he falls over four hundred feet to the rocks below.

"I landed on my back with the glider beneath me," he says. "And I guess the angle at which the frame impacted broke my fall. It was like that feeling of falling in a dream," he adds.

"You can die dreaming," Elke offers, "if you don't wake before you hit."

"Straighten up and fly right," Nick rejoins, "else your wings will go down. Or so my father always warned me."

At the bar, Condy, a local who looks as if he walked straight out of 'The Potato Eaters', recounts his role in the rescue. He is saving hay in a field beyond the warren, when he lifts his head to see Nicolas plunging down the cliff. Carrying a length of rope for securing tramcocks, Condy reaches the tower a half-hour later. Once there, he manages, for all his bulk, to descend far enough to throw Nick a line, hauling him a few yards beyond the reach of the filling tide, before walking back down from the tower to organise a boat to lift Nick off the rocks. I marvel at Condy's descent, only to learn from Roddy the publican there was in fact no better man for the job. Condy who as a lad had sleepwalked along these cliffs, robbing nests of the gulls' eggs that his mother used to find mornings on the kitchen table.

A crippled *luftmensch*, Nick sits there as if, truly made of air, he can feel no pain. Only his colour gives him away, pale as milk, tiny beads of sweat along his brow. Shortly after, Elke reports that a villager has retrieved the van. As the doctor is not to be found, Nick suggests she drive him to the hospital some hours away in Sligo Town. I propose accompanying them—to Sligo and beyond—but Nick says to stay put, that I have unfinished business here.

And so my company departs Glenmore. Elke's horn sits askance as she takes the wheel—its jaunty angle suggesting she too is for the moment out of jeopardy. Birds of a feather, she and Nicolas having both assayed what the poet who wrote so tellingly of flight once termed 'the cliffs of fall'. A week later, fragments of the birdplane wash up on the strand, a tattered wing trailing a length of cable. That same evening I tease a cloud of blond hair from my brush. Absence makes the heart grow heavier, melancholy setting in with the summer's end.

Once again upon a time or no, it takes me some months to stitch together the entire story. In October Roddy tells of another son who years ago fared ill on those same heights. Whose father took him some distance down the cliff, leaving him there to signal the herring shoals to the boat his father shortly brought round below. When rain set in, the lad panicked at the prospect of scaling the wet rockface. The father beached the boat, and eventually reached the tower where he descended in the dying light. Strapping his son to his back, he climbed back up. A year later the lad fell to his death at that very place, trying for a gull's nest a few yards below the edge.

I hunt for further clues into winter, like those who once used a long wire to probe the bog here, divining for buried oak or fir. In January Nick himself supplies a small piece of the puzzle. Enough so that I wonder that 'Landscape with Icarus' did not hang above us in the pub last August, framed under fly-specked glass. Certainly Brueghel's landscape is not entirely unlike Glenmore: sea claiming half the canvas, distant cliffs, two legs showing on the son disappearing into the drink. However it happens the painting was not hanging in the pub— rather reproduced on a postcard from Nick, postmarked from Brussels on New Year's Day. A scribbled line reports that, limbs mended, he's in Belgium on his father's business.

I scan the painting in detective fashion, noting the discrepancies, changes if you like. It is spring on the Aegean, not harvest time, and your peasant handles a plough, not scythe. A shepherd and fisherman also feature, though our Condy in fact wears both those hats in season. Were Brueghel's dun horse white, she might do for a unicorn, often mistaken for a mare by those lacking in vision. Brueghel's shepherd looks up as if something has caught his eye, but the ploughman and angler see only the tasks at hand. 'No plough stops for a dying man,' the proverb tells us, and I've heard how Irish fisherman were once loath to aid any man who fell into the sea, fearful of flying in the face of Providence. And hadn't that local lad fallen at the very spot from which his father had rescued him?

Yet myth need not be taken literally, which in Nick's case is just as well. Going to the source, I track down a copy of Ovid to read over the winter. Tales to do with changes: men and women transfigured into bird and beast, transformed into flower and stone. Echoes of the Glenmore woman who turned into a hare to steal her neighbour's cream, or the Glenmore man who bewitched a stalk of ragwort into a pig to sell at the Carrick Fair. Too despondent this weather to paint much at all, I pen-and-ink a herd of Friesians, lamely entitled 'Cow Confusion'. These cows come home, I return to hats that variously change into cones, horns, and sometimes towers.

Spring comes to Glenmore, but my interior season, masquerading as a perpetual winter, lags behind. The moral of the story I research—if anything, to fly a middle course—suggests a path between melancholy and holy madness, if only I could find it. One evening I read in Nietzsche of 'souls riddle-drunk and twilight happy, lured by flutes to any treacherous chasm'. I post these lines to Elke, who writes back of her own winter of sorrow, her Berlin factory-flat filled with feathers, the floor streaked with every colour of candle grease. Enclosed in her letter is a string of tiny celluloid discs, whose golds, greens, and turquoise I hang in my kitchen window.

Then, unheralded as always, a change comes—like an unexpected, if long-invited, guest. It's again late August, a balmy afternoon on which I finally find myself no longer out of phase. The very sun seems a gift after the rainy summer, swallows skimming yellow lakes of ragwort in the meadow opposite. Seated outside the cottage, I lay out the Tarot, the Hermit an obvious indicator of self. Of the major arcana only the Tower turns up, indicating an influence not long passed. The image is of lightning striking a tower on a cliff, over which a man and woman hurtle. Nicolas and Elke neatly enough, only it is arguably the tale of my tumble too.

I look up, but see no bolt from the blue across the bay, merely the sun on that chimney pot of stone. Low on funds, I have recently sold my books, Ovid among the volumes I unload, even if a few threads linger from that story. For one, what exactly prompted Condy to lift his head at that very moment? Was it a shadow against the sun, or simply chance alone? A long-ago frenzy of feathers, or only a flock of local daws? Whether or no, any puzzle this old is likely to be short a piece or two, whatever about the law of eternal return.

Inside the cottage I find Elke's gift reflecting the sunlight, casting its colours in disco-fashion across my white-washed cell. Foretelling what the Tarot has already foretold: a time for travel, a season of change. Suddenly I long for neon-lit scenes in lieu of country lanes, hats to try on beyond this solitary cowl. To stow away books, art, metaphysics, and simply get on with it.

So, after supper I set down an itinerary of sorts. First, my grandmother's village near Lubeck, houses of one room to a floor, the streets paved with blue cobblestones. Next Berlin, with its fallen blue angel, where I'll relay to Elke what Lindberg once advised 'of playing the edge casually'. If not strictly advice, a preferred flight pattern perhaps. After Berlin, I might call on Nicolas in Aix-en-Provence, check out Cezanne's mountain also. Homesickness, according to Ovid, prompted that first flight from a Cretan tower. Surely we all face that fabulous struggle to get back home?

OF SAINTS, SCHOLARS AND DOGS

I

"YOU'RE THE VERY MAN for the job," offered Maguire in a half-whisper, leaning so close that McElliot could only note how much like single buckshot his pupils were, fired into the centre of the iris. So small he surely had difficulty with the dark.

McElliot said nothing, his mind racing on to head Maguire off. Whether smuggling butter South or running sugar North, he knew his man Maguire who only last month had lost a finger. One story said throwing dynamite into the river after salmon; a different version claimed that after selling the fish to a local guesthouse, Maguire shot the finger off hunting rabbit. Either way the man was a chancer, a hustler, a bucko. Were he also in any way political, McElliot could not say.

"Myself the man?" he did say, cautiously.

"Aye," said Maguire in the same hushed voice. "I've a great idea for a story."

A dubious scheme all the same, McElliot reflected, though less likely to lead them down bog roads at midnight, headlamps dimmed. But, if relieved, he felt flattered also. Of all the plots offered authors by waitresses or taxi-men, Maguire's proposition was McElliot's first.

It was the writer's fifth summer in Donegal, stopping at an old cottage purchased with the cheque from an American magazine that paid beyond belief. If he had yet to sell that crowd a second story, the cottage welcoming him each July sustained in McElliot an abiding, albeit seasonal, flush of success. What was more, he did well enough with the locals. From Dublin, he had travelled widely and lived abroad, no doubt seemed more a foreigner than Irish to his neighbours in Doonalt. Blessed with magnificent mountains that tumbled to the sea, the village saw a good deal of visitors during the summer months, especially now that an armed peace had broken out across the Border sixty miles east.

That McElliot wrote for a living made little impact on his neighbours—until the past winter when a story of his appeared in a Dublin paper. A harmless tale, recounting a feud between two brothers that brought them both before the court. The bones of the story McElliot had exhumed from a provincial paper down South, Kerry or Cork, but the setting was obviously Doonalt, only thinly disguised, and the villagers had passed the paper around.

"Written by the fellow who bought John Joe's place," they informed those who hadn't McElliot's name.

When he returned to Doonalt that summer, the author sensed a certain shift in the wind. "God bless you, Mr McElliot," intoned Bernard Carr whenever the two men met, never failing to remind McElliot of some favour he'd done for the writer on his first visit there. "It wouldn't do to leave *you* standing there," remarked Paddy the Post, who now stopped his green van to lift McElliot along the road into the shops.

McElliot himself liked to fancy the favouring breeze sprang from a lingering trace of that ancient respect for the wandering bard. Like a good deal of respect, a consideration founded greatly on fear. Spurned, a poet might retaliate in verse and rhyme, dubious imitations of immortality his revenge. "God bless you to leave me out of your stories!" seemed to be more Bernard's plea.

Being only human, McElliot found some pleasure in all of this, found himself turning toward Maguire with greater warmth.

"A story is it?"

"Aye," said Maguire, wasting no time. "A woman mad with religion. Killing children before they reach the age of reason."

"To make saints of them," he finished, eyes fixed on McElliot.

Although the writer scarcely nodded, his companion, like a dog encouraged by crumbs, shifted even closer.

"She goes to the rail at every Mass. A daily Communicant, so there's no suspicion on her. She does in a dozen before they're on to her!"

"And how *do* they get on to her?" McElliot asked, more appalled than flattered by the offerings of Maguire's muse. A faraway memory surfaced somewhere at the back of his head, tales told by the Sisters, of Filipino children tortured by Japs during the last war. To renounce their faith, the nuns explained, detailing the slivers of bamboo employed by the heathen soldiers.

"Is it the priest?" queried Maguire in turn, who apparently hadn't worked out this wrinkle in the plot as yet. "He has it from her in Confession ... but he can't use that, of course ... Maybe in a moment of passion?" he suggested with a leer, wee pupils like ball bearings.

It wouldn't do at all, the editor within McElliot observed to himself. She would scarcely confess if she considered herself to be creating saints. And his man Maguire was making a balls of it, serving up a side-dish of sex along with murder. An old woman making both Saints and the Parish Priest, was it? Too many English tabloids for his companion he could only conclude. The once-banned *News of the World*, solace of the Borstal Boy in British gaols, now flogged outside Irish churches after Sunday Mass. Telefís Éireann headed rapidly down the same road.

"I doubt that kind of writing would go down well in Ireland," he told Maguire with a laugh, half-surprised at his own prudishness.

"Not to worry! It's all EU at the moment, with the Euro on its way in. No problem at all, at all!"

"Well, you should get on with it, so."

"I couldn't write home," Maguire said. If annoyed, not fooled in the slightest by McElliot's seeming obtuseness. "I'm nothing with words, only I'm giving you the idea."

"And is it your own?" McElliot asked, a hint of the law colouring his tone, as if copyright were suddenly his sole concern.

"It is, indeed," Maguire said. "'Sure they're saints in heaven,' remarks the wife the day those three young sisters died in a Dublin fire. Gives me the idea herself, she does. It's automatic, you know, provided you're under seven years of age." This in a helpful tone, in the event there were points of doctrine as well as law that might be holding McElliot back.

Like a free pass into the pictures the writer mused; only better, to hear Maguire tell it. "It would be handy all right," he said aloud, for the other's benefit. "Save all the bother, expense of canonization." Unearthing miracles, sending petitions to Rome. Never mind countless prayers to Heaven. Did they still engage an *Advocatus Diaboli* he wondered?

Sometime in the Seventies Ireland had celebrated the canonization of Blessed Oliver. What McElliot chiefly recalled was Papal praise of Plunkett—drawn, quartered, and beheaded—as "a model of reconciliation". No doubt he had obeyed like a corpse—precisely what the Jesuits asked of their own. Perhaps it was all best apprehended through irony, approached as one would Matt Talbot's Bar in Boston, named after the reformed-alcoholic Dublin ascetic, even now rumoured to be Ireland's next Saint. A dive full of rugby players scrumming to a rock & roll band the evening McElliot had dropped in. Not a hairshirt to be seen or felt.

Irony, however, was not Matt Maguire's strong suit. No subtle shifts or unexpected turns (unless possibly down a bog road to beat the law) need apply here. Nothing but the strong sell. "We could flesh it out, I suppose," McElliot offered accordingly. "A chapter for every manner of demise. One for drowning, another for poison." The entire undertaking suddenly so unreal, he gave in utterly to his collaborator, suggesting suffocation and dismemberment as if he were selecting wallpaper patterns.

"There you are!" shouted Maguire, catching a glimpse of his own genius in the mirror of McElliot's enthusiasm. "Film and TV rights!" he ejaculated, caught up in the flush.

"And your interest in it?" the literary agent within McElliot asked.

"Twenty-five per cent."

"I thought it was running butter you were about," the writer confided in a confidential tone.

"Ach, the fecking CAP has put an end to that," Maguire groused. "No bloody money to be made in groceries now at all."

It was high time he got down to work again, McElliot told himself on the road home. His latest story, a day in the life of a museum guard in Madrid, finished over a month ago. Though he hadn't enlightened Maguire on the subject, the story of the two brothers which the village had seen that winter was one of few ever set in Ireland. The majority unfolded rather in locales like Amsterdam and San Francisco, even Athens or Istanbul. All a good distance from Doonalt, nor was it a matter of miles alone.

Still, for all the absurdity of Maguire's yarn, there was in McElliot's work a contrasting lack of imagination. A sense of something missing which was at best only partially obscured by the foreign, sometimes exotic setting. Editors who praised his eye for detail cited the absence of something else, putting words on it that ranged from 'conflict' to 'compulsion'. No one went so far as to accuse him of substituting topography for inspiration however, and he surely sold enough work to be considered successful in a modest way. More money than in groceries at any rate, he chuckled to himself, pausing at his gate to note the moonlight like spotlamps on sheep in the field below.

The memory of Maguire's mad woman tagged after McElliot the next day, like a headache from too much drink. There was correspondence to answer, a few clothes to wash, nothing demanding enough to bar the mind's door entirely against her. Passing up the pub that night, he began a murder mystery purchased in the shop next to the Chapel.

By the following day McElliot could see her features as clearly as if he had dreamt them. She was no caricature as Maguire might have drawn her, all streaming hair and frantic eyes. Rather her face was on the long side, though short of horsy, the flesh still firm for her age which McElliot gauged to be somewhere over seventy. Short in stature, she stood slightly stooped at the shoulder, dressed in a black skirt with a scarlet cardigan over a black top. The skirt was dusty with turf ash, the sweater holed at the elbows.

She appeared again the next morning in the same outfit, which he guessed she probably wore for days on end. He wondered now if that were how long she intended to stay on, grateful she was at least the silent type. Unable to work, he began another paperback detective, not a female over twenty-five in its world of crime.

As he boiled an egg for his tea that evening McElliot managed a closer look, remarking in her eyes perhaps the first clue to her condition. It was nothing as facile as a demented gaze: more a flicker of real pain beneath depths of sadness, like the glimmer of goldfish at the bottom of a garden pond. Or was said simile itself too much a garden variety? he mused—before recoiling with a start that suggested his fish had metaphorized into something worse.

"There's no bloody need for tropes of any kind!" he shouted aloud. Nor would he write a word of it down. She was Maguire's old woman, not his, and clearly she had worn her welcome out. If McElliot had been initially curious, it had been in a suitably professional manner, as disinterested as a doctor with a patient. But as he had no intention of writing her story, it now felt somewhat akin to eavesdropping—though she had yet to utter a single word. More like peering through a window at an old woman—a practice likely to prove more distasteful yet.

Halfway through his egg he saw that her latest manifestation offered him a clue to her origins. Above her mouth there was a small mole with several whiskers, resembling a birthmark on his elder sister's face. Summoning the old woman to mind, he remarked this time a likeness in the line of her jaw to his younger sister. As the outline of the familiar upon awakening eases a troubled sleep, a relieved McElliot saw that the face was composed to some degree of features borrowed from his two siblings, executed in the manner of a composite police sketch used to identify perpetrators of violent crime. Juxtaposing this nose with that moustache until the victim had his (or her) man.

Having espied the familiar—nay, familial—in her physiognomy, McElliot banished the old woman at once. Grateful for their intercession, he would write his sisters in the morning. Acknowledge the card which had annoyed him upon its arrival the previous week, picturing the Swiss Guards at the Vatican in full dress. Annoyed him because it was at least five years since their last pilgrimage to Rome, where they had apparently purchased a great reserve of postcards.

The cards still tracked McElliot down from time to time, Michelangelo's *Moses* or St Peter's Square, all bearing the postmark of the small English village near Bristol where they had moved from Dublin years before. It was not the Italian art which irritated him. Rather its ecclesiastical content, his sisters having grown increasingly religious over the years, as if to compensate for his own drift from the Church. To McElliot their cards were too much like notices from his dentist in the post, colourful reminders of Divine Appointments made on his behalf.

The latest card told of a trip to London for a rally. How moving it had been: 100,000 gathered there; they'd had lemonade on the train in. They were as vague as that, but McElliot gathered from an English paper left by a visitor in the pub that it had been an anti-abortion protest, though according to the paper his sisters had been other than conservative in their estimate of the crowd.

"A rally?" he would write them, feigning ignorance. "I didn't know you were political?" though that wasn't entirely true either. "You know we have a soft spot in our heart for Franco," they had written him during the despot's dying days: the stability of Europe for his sisters having little to do with common markets or currency links. "Hasn't he stood like a bastion against Communism for all these years?" they had penned on a black & white card of the Catacombs.

At breakfast the old woman was back, dogging McElliot with an authority that sent him fleeing for the dictionary.

"Autochthonous," he half-remembered aloud, and he was right at that, only confusion as to its spelling had him searching for several minutes. *Indigenous as in rocks* read the first definition, but it was psychology, not geology, he wanted:

> *adj. 2. Pertaining to ideas which arise apart from an individual's train of thought, seeming to have some alien or external agency as their source.*

He pondered its hint of the subversive, its seeming allusion, even, to his sisters' least-favourite change-agents, namely outside agitators and the KGB. In any event, his visitor was no longer just Maguire's woman any more. Nor had his sisters all that much to do with her, he accepted this morning, beyond a few minor details. And even there he had observed how the woman's upper lip with its mole sometimes quivered. Like a rabbit he thought, something that neither sister had ever resembled.

Nor was it any longer like eavesdropping. Instead the woman now followed him, from scullery to bedroom to study, managing the step up or down between every room. "You might at least help with the washing-up," he told her after dinner, though it was well past the point where feeble humour might set the situation right. Hagiography was not his strong suit; obsession nothing he had ever cared to tackle in his writing—something better left to the Russians. Unable to work, he wondered if he were not being unravelled by the woman as one undoes a knitted jumper, pulling all the while on a single thread. As if to reassure him, the old woman began to knit by an open fire, a faded picture of the Scared Heart above the hearth.

After supper McElliot took a walk along the strand. Following the ribbon of wrack unwound by the tide, he found his fine eye for detail turned morbid also, descrying nothing but decay in the debris flung up by the sea. Impermanence everywhere but the scraps of coloured plastic, which time itself would not touch.

Retrieving a sheep's skull from the sand, he saw the withered membrane of its nasal cavity stir in the breeze, sere like an autumn leaf. "You're in a bad way, mate," he said aloud, before turning back.

In the days following, McElliot tried to make a story of it after all, settling on Agnes for a name. "Exorcism, I suppose," he muttered, only it didn't seem to take. Refusing confinement to the typewritten page, Agnes preferred to ghost round the cottage, taking every opportunity to throw herself across the tracks of his train of thought. As if agreeing that Maguire had offered only melodrama for motivation, the old woman tried to help McElliot herself, speaking up at last.

"Modern times," she said at breakfast, her host buried in the Dublin daily he bought out of loyalty for the story they had published. "'Tis to save them from times such as these."

It was of small use to him, her words merely echoing the despair that had washed over McElliot since his walk along the strand. As if the morbidity midst wrack and flotsam now coloured all that he saw, even his newspaper which of late seemed little more than a daily catalogue of deprivation and atrocity.

That morning's headlines told of a small Belfast boy killed by a letter bomb. Unable to finish the story, he turned to finer type relating the arrival of a major relic at St Oliver's birthplace, his left femur bone to be precise. Among Letters to the Editor he read a lengthy epistle dismissing the hazards of nuclear waste, a shorter missive warning of certain risks to hygiene in licking postal stamps. Not prepared to take a stand on either issue, he nonetheless found their juxtaposition evidence enough the world was utterly out of whack.

"'Tis the age we live in," she whispered again across the table.

It was a start, he supposed, though he knew he wasn't the man for the job. Seated once in the Abbey Theatre beside an elderly country man, McElliot had noted how the old fellow recoiled, even groaned aloud, whenever the decrepit crone from the play came scolding onstage. His peasant acceptance of the old woman's reality, not unlike the credence once granted the Devil in a morality play, left McElliot wishing he might create fictional characters with half that impact.

Now faced with such a task, he found himself unequal to it. The years of flying from Venice to Vienna, countless cappuchinos in continental cafés—all of it had immersed him too deeply in modern times, rendering him unfit for what felt more like a medieval undertaking. Lacking even his sisters' faith, he sensed it would take something stronger than lemonade to look upon the world as Agnes did. Nor was it healthy or human, he believed, to embrace all the sorrows of creation as Agnes had. One wanted to keep a historical perspective in mind. With slots for commercial messages, as in TV documentaries on the World Wars or the Holocaust, he told himself, shuddering at the sudden memory of a schoolmate who cut off his hand one Sunday after Mass: the text Matthew, Chapter V, on casting out the sinning eye.

He was prone of late to such violent attacks of memory, as sharp as the bamboo splinters employed in the martyrdom of Filipino youth. Spasms like one which landed him back in his schoolyard on the morning he had arrived first of all the scholars: to find a dead rabbit jammed through the door-handle, its headless torso twisted there like a rag to stop the draught.

Sunday morning he rose to find his melancholy shifted, the sluggish swell on his interior sea replaced by a high wind and surging waves. He tore out of bed to prepare a breakfast large enough for two, dropping the tea-ball in the teapot like a depth-charge, which set the water to roil and tumble as air escaped below. Washing the delft, he felt the power of imagination sweeping him along like the California surf, conflict and compulsion as near to hand as the salt and pepper on his breakfast table.

Agnes however had failed to appear, having slept in he decided. Still seated at the table, he caught himself calculating the ages of the children he could see out the window, returning from Mass, trying to gauge who was not yet seven. When evening brought no relief he set out for the pub, worried that he was coming entirely unstuck. As he passed the long meadow sloping seaward from the road, McElliot recalled a Christmas visit to Donegal, a farmer piling turf and straw on a large rock in the middle of the field, keeping a fire smoldering day and night, so that a bucket of cold water one morning would split the rock asunder.

Taking a stool beneath the TV, he ordered a bottle of stout. Bernard Carr came over for a chat, of which McElliot held up his end with surprising success. "God bless you," Bernard offered in parting as Maguire came in the door, making McElliot reflect it was himself who had more cause to fear the locals than vice-versa. He watched Maguire settle in beside the fire, next to Paddy the Post. Full of mail-fraud schemes without a doubt.

The TV then came on above him. Looking up, McElliot felt as if he were underwater, peering at figures in a green sea overhead. The picture focused as the evening news began, opening with film footage of the funeral that morning in Belfast, the small boy killed by the letter bomb. The camera showed the procession with wee casket down a crowded street, a close-up of mourners on a corner. Suddenly a grey-haired woman filled the screen, lifting what looked her grandson, not five years old, above her head so that he might see the cortège.

The lad looked merely puzzled, but it was the woman who held McElliot's eye. Her face was contorted and she was shouting. The audio was broken up, yet half-reading her lips, he made out something about saints and martyrs, the child in her arms beginning to cry. With that, the picture turned sea-green again, and the pub itself began to spin. Gazing wildly around the room he wondered had Maguire seen their woman, mad with religion, making martyrs and saints of mere children.

"He must be in the toilet!" he stammered aloud, turning a few heads along the bar. The faces regarding him began to spin, soon joined by others: his two sisters, a likeness of Blessed Oliver from the colour photogravure in a Sunday supplement, Generalissimo Franco, a nameless chum from primary school, Maguire putting in an appearance at last, but no sign of Agnes at all. "To be set free by the News at Nine," he marvelled, before his head began to whirl so hard he was afraid it would fly apart.

He had no memory of the road home when he woke late the next afternoon. He felt as if he had slept for days—felt utterly exhausted, yet not unfit. A cup of tea taken, he stepped from the cottage into a gentle rain. Noting to himself the sharp edge of turf smoke, acrid against the soft, amorphous air, McElliot knew he was his own man once more. More suited to contrast than conflict, he began that very evening another story. Of an Irishman who had emigrated to New Zealand. A lover of flowers, he cross-bred and perfected countless hybrids, trying for years to create a perfectly black rose. Time and time again a black bud formed, only to have a crimson stain seep always in as the petals slowly blossomed.

IT WAS PADDY THE POST who brought McElliot the bad news. "I hear Dog Doyle's gunning for you," he announced, handing over a phone bill. "What's up with Dog?" McElliot replied, annoyed there was nothing from his agent. "The poem you wrote with him in it," Paddy said flatly, as if delivering a summons.

"I don't write poems," McElliot replied, thinking the postman was only trying to put the wind up him. "It hadn't your name on it," Paddy conceded, "but Doyle claims it was you wrote it all the same."

Suddenly the postman had McElliot's attention. "What poem are we on about?" he snapped, stomach churning. "Did you not see the *Sunday Indo*?" Paddy smiled. "'The Ballad of Mad Dog Doyle'?"

An invisible cloud edged across the sun as the postal van drove off. Libel is a liability for any writer, but even McElliot had never dreamt of being hoist on another scribbler's petard. Indoors, he found the arts section from the paper in the fridge, wrapped around a nice-sized pollock taken off the rocks the previous evening. McElliot read the *Sunday Indo*, but skipped its books page which had recently panned his own work. A hatchet job in fact, laced with the kind of tripe that passed these days for Dublin wit.

Turning the sodden pages, he saw it was a Dublin poet who had done the job on Doyle—the very Dublin poet whom McElliot had brought to Dog's door. Groaning at the memory of that misstep, he read quickly on. There were only a few lines from the poem about Doyle in a review of the Poet's latest book, but the Poet had cited Doonalt as well, sticking a pin on the map in case Ireland boasted two Doyles named Dog.

A Dog by name as by nature, McElliot read, *a vulpine cunning has this craythur!* Safe enough with *vulpine*, the Poet had nonetheless failed to recast Dog Doyle as, let's say, Bull Boyle, and thereby cover his tracks. The rest of it was even worse: the smoky interior of Dog's cottage evoking, for the Poet, the shadows in Plato's cave! It was, McElliot felt, enough to sicken your arse, though naturally the reviewer loved it, citing the Poet's 'gift for bridging Ireland's rural/urban divide'.

"More a gift for placing others at risk," McElliot grumbled, going over to lock the kitchen door. "Oh, there'll be bits of skin and hair flying yet!" Paddy the Post had laughed, getting into his van.

A Dubliner himself, McElliot had worked hard to fit into his adopted Donegal village. At first he was known simply as "the fellow who bought John Joe's place". "Sure, that cottage's only a novelty to him," they said as McElliot came and went, until the writer finally settled into Doonalt year-round. Always lifting neighbours along the road, never failing to buy a round in the pub, McElliot found himself gradually accepted for what he was.

A provisional acceptance, to be sure, given that McElliot was, after all, a writer. "I think twice before I speak once to you," Biddy the Shop often reminded him. "Put mouth to mouth, but don't put pen to paper," Maloney the Pub cautioned another evening, after which McElliot took care to conceal the small notebook he always carried.

At the same time, being a writer brought with it a certain licence. "People expect eccentricities of an artist," explained Maloney, who had read a book or two himself. "Like smoking two cigarettes at once, or having three wives." McElliot, a single non-smoker, resolved thereafter to worry less about how he might be fitting in. That he missed Mass most Sundays was only what might be expected of him. And should he ever go mouth to mouth with a Doonalt woman, he need not fret over what the village made of that!

Indeed its rugged coastal beauty had brought Doonalt a number of artists over the years—not all of whom had, according to local lights, done the locale proud. Per Paddy the Post, an American painter who once summered there alluded in his memoirs to the fleas in his bed. A renowned English composer was similarly remembered for having cited the greasy table in his holiday lodging. Apprised of these sensitivities, McElliot took care in his writing not to run afoul of local sensibilities. "You won't make a postcard of me," Jimmy the Bog warned off any camera-toting tourist who came upon him cutting turf. Yet for all McElliot's precautions, here he now stood: charged with having made poetry out of Doonalt's Dog Doyle!

Getting up, he unlocked the kitchen door, deciding it unlikely Doyle would come after him on a bright breezy April day, ideal for the bog. Moreover the flimsy lock would scarcely deter Dog. "You must be six-foot tall?" the writer had inquired some years before of a hulking local in Maloney's pub. "Only Our Lord was six-foot," replied Dog Doyle, turning a bloodshot eye on McElliot. "Any man else is at least a quarter-inch off." "I didn't know that," the writer conceded, calculating Doyle carried some fifteen stone on his six-foot-and-a-fraction frame.

The hard life however had taken its toll on Doyle. "He's come down a lot," Sergeant Haynes remarked another night in the pub. "It would bring a horse down," replied Maloney, who often urged a bowl of soup on Doyle. "The apple doesn't fall far from the orchard," Bernard Carr observed, recalling Dog's da who used to carry the odd dead sheep off the mountain and roast it over the coals. Should a calf leave any milk in its bucket, the elder Doyle would lift it up and swallow all.

The talk turned then to a minor scandal occasioned by Dog after an all-night hooley at the small hotel above the bay the summer before. Bound for early Mass the next morning, Maloney the Pub had come upon Matt the Melodeon and Dog Doyle headed home. Matt looked a little worn but Dog, jacket torn and shirt-tail trailing, was a holy show. "Have sense, men," Maloney cautioned, urging them to take the lower road and thereby eschew the crowd outside the chapel door. "I know what you mean, only the grass is wet," snapped Dog, striding up the hill and past the assembled faithful.

Oddly enough, McElliot and Doyle had over time struck up a kind of acquaintance. Perhaps Doyle saw in the writer a fellow free-spirit? Or possibly a fellow traveller, though Dog had spent only a single year in Glasgow, whereas McElliot had sojourned as far afield as Athens and Alexandria. Glasgow in 1938 had left an impression on Doyle however, who marvelled yet at his former digs in a hostel above the Clyde. "What beds didn't fit into rooms went in the hallways. The place full of World War I veterans," he reminisced, "living on pensions. Half of 'em missing an ear or a nose!"

For his part, the writer discovered in Doyle a wealth of idiosyncrasy that helped shorten the long winter nights. Slipping onto an adjacent stool, McElliot would listen as Dog discoursed on the dozen dead Russian cosmonauts, still circling overhead like so many human satellites. Or how a child raised entirely without language would grow up speaking Hebrew!

Whatever the bond between them, McElliot never presumed so far as to inquire of Dog the etymology of his Christian name. "How is it that you are called Nehru?" he once innocently inquired of a neighbouring farmer. "There'll be a solicitor's letter in the post to you," responded Nehru, "the very day that name ever appears in print." Such naming was commonplace in rural Ireland, but in Doonalt it appeared to be practiced with a vengeance. Some appellations—such as Peter the Meter (who read the electricity) or Brian the Bread (with his van of loaves)—merely nodded at a vocation, much as Chandler or Cooper once signified. Others—like Jack Flukes or Barney Bush—proved more elusive. In fact—not Bush but *Busch*—as McElliot finally learned: Barney first in Doonalt to acquire a radio of that manufacture. According to Maloney, Nehru was given to barratry in most matters; nevertheless McElliot took care thereafter with nomenclature—unlike the Poet who hadn't the wit to render Dog Doyle as Hog Coyle. As for the derivation of Dog, McElliot credited the two or three curs skulking in Doyle's wake whenever he left his cottage up the mountain.

Two autumns ago McElliot had visited that very cottage, accompanied by the Painter, an old schoolmate, who had landed at McElliot's the previous night with the Poet in tow. A loud hammering on his door had awakened McElliot, who did not mask his irritation at being dragged from his bed. Merry with drink, the Painter and the Poet fell to frying a feed of fish purchased en route, farting all the while as if their bowels were true wind instruments. A pot of bloody fish heads greeted McElliot in the scullery next morning, the air heavy with the oily smell of grilled mackerel.

"How's your head?" the Poet inquired repeatedly at breakfast, as if his host's pate were a chronic complaint, an old war injury like the missing noses on Dog Doyle's vets. "How's your head?" he asked, smacking his lips as he shovelled in porridge under a straggly moustache.

"How's your knee?" McElliot wanted to snarl back. "How's your fecking arse?" Later, having borrowed McElliot's fishing rod, the Poet lost its tackle on seawrack along the bottom. Returning to the cottage, he paused in Nehru's meadow just long enough to relieve himself, pissing in plain view of the entire parish.

"I've a painting in the Ballyshannon Arts Festival," the Painter explained at lunch. "Where that bollocks," indicating the Poet who was polishing off the plum preserves, "was reading his poems. Fed up and far from home, we decided to track you down!"

In fact McElliot was fond of the Painter, whom he admired for having none of his own innate caution. Taught by Christian Brothers in a building overrun with rats, the two lads had copied out French conjugations assigned by a half-mad Brother who manned a fishing line which ran from his desk out to the hall, its huge cod hook baited with a lump of greasy meat. Returning once from the toilet, the Painter tugged sharply on the line, ducking down the hall as the Brother flew out, waving a wooden mallet.

At university the two friends took rooms together. During those years the Painter introduced McElliot to the West of Ireland, dragging him along on rainy weekends to Connemara. Or Kerry, where their motley band of would-be bohemians hiked the rolling hills, stumbling back at night from the pub to sodden tents inevitably pitched in a muddy pasture. Indeed it was the memory of those outings that prompted McElliot years later to purchase a cottage in mountainy Donegal.

Highly regarded as a younger artist, the Painter never delivered on his early promise. These days he earned his crust by dashing off sentimental landscapes for a Dublin furniture dealer, who flogged them with sitting-room suites to the emerging Irish bourgeoisie. Each painting which brought forty pounds took two hours only to execute, leaving the Painter ample time in which to neglect any serious art. "I suspect prostitution has its price," he told McElliot in Maloney's on the second night.

Drinking pints by the fire, the two friends recalled a weekend in Kerry their last year of university. Despite the circumstantial evidence of a pool table, the Dingle barman had insisted there were no balls. Undeterred, the Painter and two companions commenced to play, calling each shot and clicking their tongues whenever the intangible cue ball pocketed an equally immaterial solid or striped. A few locals gathered to watch the game, offering advice and applauding any especially

deft stroke. Unnerved by the carry-on, the barman finally
hoisted the table at one end, effectively scattering the balls.

Things didn't get as out of hand that evening in Maloney's,
though lively enough. Struck by an uncanny resemblance, the
same bald head and piercing eyes, the Painter inquired of a
local named Molloy had he ever heard of Picasso? "Sure,
wasn't I called that in London years ago," replied Molloy, who
had actually worked as a house painter there. "Are you called
that here?" asked the Painter. "Feck it, who in Doonalt ever
heard of Picasso?" Molloy snorted in disgust.

"You've a grand village here," the Painter told McElliot,
returning to the fire with a small one in either hand. Meantime
the Poet, whose round it had been, stood between Paddy the
Post and Dog Doyle, bellowing a song like a lovesick heifer.
When McElliot next looked, the Poet was leaping to and fro,
simulating the swordplay that featured in another ballad of star-
crossed love. McElliot looked on warily, knowing the locals
loved to put a pig's head on a stranger, yet the crowd in
Maloney's only smiled their delight as the Poet hurtled about
like a March hare. Drinks were subsequently ordered all
around, and when Sergeant Haynes appeared at closing time,
the three Dubliners accepted Dog Doyle's invitation to follow
him home.

Two days after Paddy the Post tipped him off, McElliot drove
into Ballybegs where he found a copy of the Poet's latest
collection in the bookshop above the pier. After reading the
poem on Doyle, he replaced the book and bought one by
himself, a stratagem he occasionally practiced to suggest a
demand for the stuff.

As he drove home, McElliot conceded the Poet clearly hadn't set out to skin Dog Doyle. Lord knows, there was plenty about Dog that wasn't in the poem. Take, for example, the half-ounce of tobacco he always chewed at Mass without spitting once. "No worry of worms!" Maloney the Pub had whispered to McElliot in the pew behind. Besides, what the Poet *had* described was accurate enough, not least the miserable fire of sally branches and wet turf Dog had lit that night, useless against the autumn chill. Stumbling over his dogs, Doyle had next attempted to rustle up some grub, throwing a cup of water and a greasy rasher into a blackened pan, setting a grey lump of Stork margarine and half a sliced pan upon the table.

In the end nobody had bothered with food. Instead the Poet poured vodka into lager—what the Painter termed 'loony soup' before falling off his own chair. Shortly after, Dog took a notion the Poet was in fact some class of spy. "You wouldn't believe the Rosary from that fellow," he informed McElliot, glaring across at the Poet who was by then beyond speech. "There's more in that head than a comb would take out," Dog snarled, disappearing into the lower room with a crash.

"One spider knows another," countered McElliot as the room began to spin. There was no sign of Doyle the next morning, as his guests staggered down the lane. The Painter and Poet departed Doonalt that afternoon, the latter likely already casting a lyrical eye on the previous evening.

Back from the bookshop in Ballybegs, McElliot stopped at Maloney's to report on the full text of 'The Ballad of Mad Dog

Doyle'. "I imagine accuracy is no defence," he asked the publican, "once you put someone in a poem?"

"There's two things people don't like hearing about themselves," agreed Maloney. "Lies and the truth."

"Whatever you say, say nothing," said McElliot, keeping an eye on the door for Doyle.

"Wasn't it Newman," Maloney poured himself a small one, "who suggested the futility of attempting a sinless literature on sinful man?"

"Aye, paper never refused ink," rejoined McElliot, fingering the plastic bag of 5p pieces he now carried in his pocket, just small enough to fit inside his fist. If the pen were truly mightier than the sword, a stout stick would be handier yet.

"There's less risk in painting," McElliot posited two pints later, confident Doyle would not appear that evening. "Take Velasquez," he informed Maloney, who was pouring Picasso Molloy a rum and black. "Who got paid for painting his patrons to look like eejits!"

"Could you get away with painting a Doonalt woman naked?" leered Picasso, not the least interested in his fellow Spanish painter.

"Composites would be safe enough," retorted McElliot. "Teresa's thighs, Agnes' arse, and Brigid's breasts!"

"There'll come nothing wholesome from that pen," Maloney declared, bringing it back to the Poet. "A bad article, that fellow."

"Cute as a Christian," trumpeted McElliot, flushed by the continual administration of stimulants.

A week later Dog Doyle caught up to him. At the mobile bank, which stopped each Monday outside Maloney's. The large blue van was roomy within, yet the villagers treated it like a confessional, waiting their turn outside lest they overhear a neighbour's bank balance.

"What is it exactly you write?" inquired Maeve that afternoon behind her counter.

"Bank drafts and bad cheques," jested McElliot, who rather fancied the teller.

"Out of date and out of danger," smiled Maeve, making the writer wonder should he ask her out?

Descending the van steps, McElliot saw Doyle lying in wait.

"Go to the bank and draw your breath!" barked Dog by way of greeting.

"How's Dog?" McElliot queried in true Donegal fashion.

"You're a right stocking of tripe," snapped Doyle.

"Easy now," McElliot cautioned.

"You walked me into it," Dog closed in. "Making money off my good name."

"I never made a penny off you," McElliot stepped back.

"Arraff, aren't you after lodging it?" bayed Doyle, aiming a mad slap at the writer's ear.

"Have sense, man!" McElliot sidestepped, as if sense had ever been in Dog's curriculum. He was too slow however and Doyle caught him by the coat. Arms extended, Dog waltzed the Dubliner around the van, attempting to work a calloused thumb into McElliot's eye, his knee already pulverising the writer's privates. Struggling to keep his feet, McElliot sensed, for all his terror, a kind of epiphany to hand, its instrument the same Dog Doyle whose elbow was halfway down his throat.

"Man bites Dog!" laughed Picasso in the pub that night, describing Doyle's yelp of pain just as Sergeant Haynes had arrived.

"Films have been made of a lesser day," declared Paddy the Post, standing the badly bruised writer a pint.

"Had he kept ahold of me, I was finished," summed up McElliot, signalling Maloney to pour the postman a small one in return.

"It wouldn't do to book Dog," Haynes the Law had counselled McElliot after breaking up the fight. "Have his name in the *Democrat* for all to read?"

"I've no intention of pressing charges," McElliot assured the Sergeant, "provided Doyle keeps himself on a short lead."

As to his own part in the debacle, McElliot would plead not guilty but submit to the facts. The secondary use of facts a writer, like a magpie, collects: the bits and scraps of other lives from which a story is fashioned. Moreover, thanks to his *danse absurde* with Dog, a sidelines seat would no longer suffice. Trapped in Doyle's avid embrace, clasped as it were to humanity's very bosom—with all its passions and attendant sour smells—McElliot felt lucky to have escaped with his life. Having done so, he no longer felt content to play the perennial observer; rather he burned now with the desire to write solely from experience, to spin it out of his belly like a spider, no more the fly upon the wall. What's more, he suddenly sensed to hand a story line that just might snare a certain Poet in its web!

Leaving his stool, McElliot dodged into the toilet to jot down a few notes for precisely such a tale. His notebook tucked away, he returned to the bar feeling jauntier than he had in weeks. "Shaw, an Irishman, believed there are two kinds of people," he hailed the Sergeant at closing time. "Those who can stop two Dogs fighting, and those who cannot!"

SHOE THE DONKEY

MAGGIE WOKE TO A MAGPIE scolding on the wire fence above the earthen bank at the back of the cottage. The same fence over which Neddy had brayed at their bedroom window any morning they chose to lie on after they got rid of the cow. "We should have sold that donkey too," Packy would mutter, getting out the bed. "Worse than a bloody rooster." But Maggie knew Packy didn't mean it, for he knew how fond she was of Neddy. Just as she knew he hadn't intended to dispose of the donkey in the manner he did, once she had finally accepted it made little sense to keep him any longer. What's more, she sensed this morning she might at last be ready to forgive him Neddy's fate.

Packy was already up and out, footering about the byre or clearing a drain in the meadow below. "No cow, no cares," Maggie's father had often declaimed, "and a long sleep in the morning." But Packy could rarely lie on, cow or no cow. Rather he worked hard to find work about the farm—now the farming was finished up. The sheep had been first to go, Packy no longer fit to run after Shay over the hill, gathering them to be dipped or clipped. Or have their ears punched for the sheep bounty which was the only excuse for keeping them. And so

Packy's nephew Danny arrived one morning to drive them over the road to his own farm on the north side of the village.

A month later, Shay was killed by a car on the road.

"Would you not get a new pup?" Maggie urged Packy, if only to keep him company.

"There's no need for a dog," Packy said, "with no sheep about the place."

The magpie had flown off by the time Maggie raised the blind onto a pale blue March sky. Easter was late this year which meant Lent ran late too—allowing Maggie to lie in since Packy, fasting, took only tea and toast for breakfast. Her own father had not been so observant of Lent.

"Where's the egg?" he had demanded of her mother, staring at the cup of black tea and dry toast.

"It's Good Friday," came the reproof.

"It's a good Friday when you get an egg!" her father had snorted in disgust.

Maggie put on the kettle before stowing the two milk cartons Packy had left on the table into the tiny fridge which still seemed a novelty. Six months after the sheep departed, Packy had come down with a bad dose, having struggled through the wet summer to save enough hay to fodder the cow.

"It makes no sense," he told Maggie. "Killing yourself for a drop of milk in the tea, when a van can leave it at your door." A month later a jobber drove out from Dunbeg and loaded the cow into a lorry.

Packy kept at the turf for another year, going up to the bog far above the cottage any dry day from March on. Once he had a year's burning saved, he built a stack above the turf bank, thatched with sods and rushes and secured with several sections of old fishing net. Then, as they had done every day for twenty years, he and Neddy went up the hill, where he filled two large creels on the donkey's back.

Packy had wanted nothing to do with the turf-cutting machine when it first arrived in the parish, spitting out turf like long sodden shites. But two years after he sold the sheep, Packy conceded he had likewise grown too old for the bog. It was that same year he also began to talk about getting rid of Neddy. "It makes no sense keeping a donkey," he told Maggie the very August afternoon Danny brought a trailer-load of machine-cut turf off the hill and dumped it beside the byre.

"It makes no sense keeping a donkey," he said the following year, the very day a lorry dumped the tonne of free coal they got now that Packy had turned sixty-five. Maggie disliked coal, filthy fuel that it was, but a few lumps on top of the turf in the range on a frosty night would not go amiss. And this time she reluctantly agreed with Packy about the donkey.

She knew it was foolish to have grown attached to the beast to begin with. The kind of thing townspeople did, whereas farm folk knew better. Only her mother had been as bad, spoiling a particular heifer until it followed her around the meadow like a dog. And bellowed, lovesick, any summer night it heard her out walking the road. It was townspeople who kept cats as pets, whereas a farm family suffered them to keep rats and mice in check. Only last summer they had been plagued by a feral cat, sneaking in any open window and making a mess. Until Packy borrowed Danny's .22 and surprised it one morning by the west gable.

Packy was not happy at shooting the cat. Nor had he allowed myxomatosis onto their land. "It was the Normans who introduced the rabbit to Ireland," he informed Maggie, startling her with his knowledge. Indeed it was this softness in him that had long ago won her heart, a softness that contrasted entirely to the hardness in her father. Or in her brother Liam who at age six, after watching their father wring the neck of an old hen, had gone out and wrung the necks of the remaining five. For which her father had beat him—less for the wanton loss of life which had made Maggie cry—than for the cost of the fowl.

But at least her father wasn't outright brutal, like Master Cunnea, who would give the globe on his desk a furious spin, stopping it with a random stab of his forefinger on Alaska or Arabia.

"Where's that young Doherty?" he barked at Packy one afternoon, pointing to Siberia.

"Somewhere east of Dunbeg, sir?" Packy answered. The class laughed, waiting for the Master to give Packy a clout, but Maggie saw only the lack of guile which the others had mistaken for stupidity.

That Packy had been as upset by Neddy's fate doubtlessly helped foster the forgiveness she had sensed upon awaking. That, plus her part in making a pet out of the donkey in the first place. Though that's what Neddy had been—a pet, a large dote, with his soft lips or the flat bony bit between his eyes which he loved to have scratched. Or the musty-clean smell of him, or the way he always tried to get his nose into her cardigan pocket, whenever he smelt the bit of old apple or carrot she had for him.

"You were up early?" she said as Packy appeared in the doorway. Shedding his wellingtons, he tucked the boots neatly behind the downspout, tops folded over against a shower. "No point lying on," he said, "when you're wide awake."

"You should get some sleeping tablets off Dr Hagerty so," she teased, knowing he had never taken a tablet in his life. Nor had her father, though that had not stopped him from requesting them of Dr Galligan.

"Are ye not sleeping, Paddy?"

"Oh, it's not for me," her father had explained, "but the rats." The rats having worked their way into a potato pit behind the house, making a terrible mess. Crushing some of her mother's tablets into treacle, her father had set the concoction out for the rats, going out in the morning with a spade to finish them off. And Dr Galligan had given him more tablets too.

His cup of tea taken, Packy unfolded his wellingtons and went out for spuds for the dinner. Her father often wore his boots into the house, provided her mother were not there to bark at him. And her Packy was neater in other ways too. Like always trimming Neddy's hooves—never allowing them to curl up, as her father and Uncle Mick had done with their donkeys.

"If we can find a decent home for him," she had finally given into Packy six months before. Only it turned out nobody in the village had need of an old donkey.

"Did you try Christy Boyle?" Maggie asked.

"Christy wouldn't feed a wet hen," Packy said, "much less a donkey."

Maggie remembered reading something about a donkey sanctuary in Cork, but she knew Packy would only laugh at the idea—never mind cost—of sending an old Ulster donkey down to Munster. And so it stood for a fortnight, until the afternoon Packy returned from Dunbeg, which boasted a proper hardware store, along with five or six pubs. She was always anxious when Packy went to town, recalling how her father would come home flootered, and the row that always followed. Worse was the market day her father had taken Liam and her into a pub and bought them each a mineral. As he and Uncle Mick pushed up to the crowded bar, her father had bellowed out for all to hear: "It's not often we comes to town, lads, but when we comes to town, we comes to town!"

"I've a home for Neddy," Packy announced that afternoon, placing his messages on the kitchen table.

"A home? Where?"

"In the Russian Circus."

"The circus?" Maggie asked, astounded.

"Aye, the circus."

"What does a circus want with an old donkey?" she asked in disbelief.

"Ach, what do ye think?" Packy said, impatient with a couple of drinks in him. "He'll help putting up or taking down the tent. All manner of tasks."

"Giving rides to the weans during the interval," he added, making Maggie brighten at the prospect of a child on Neddy's back as a circus hand led them around the ring.

"Will they not work him too hard?"

"Sure, the fellah who bought him said they wouldn't work him at all."

"They bought him?" she said, astonished.

"Aye, five pounds," Packy smiled. "Plus tickets for Sunday's matinee," holding them up like a pair of aces.

Packy told her all as she prepared his tea. How he had gone into the Harbour Bar for a bottle of stout, only to fall into company with several Russians from the circus. "Just one of them spoke English," Packy explained, "but they were delighted I had a donkey going cheap."

"Will they feed him properly?" Maggie asked, unsettled at the idea of Neddy in the care of foreigners—Russians even.

"Sure, doesn't a circus travel on its stomach?" Packy said, sounding almost worldly. "And this buck was Bulgarian, not Russian," he added, confident it all lay somewhere east of Dunbeg.

Her jest that morning over the sleeping tablets was the first time Maggie had teased Packy in months—further evidence she was finally prepared to set aside the donkey's departure. Peeling carrots for their dinner, she recalled how she had fed Neddy a stone of them over the last two days. Though she had stayed inside that Saturday when Danny arrived with a horse box to take Neddy away. Not wanting to be seen brushing away tears, even if the donkey were headed to a good home.

Danny had lifted her and Packy into Dunbeg the next afternoon, dropping them at the red-and-white-striped tent pitched in a field outside the town. Their tickets were for the best seats—front row, ring centre, on folding chairs—not the benches which Maggie knew would have had her back destroyed after an hour. Seated, she kept an eye out for Neddy behind the curtain at the entrance to the ring. But when the crowd began to clap as the lights came down, leaving a large red lamp to cast its crimson everywhere, Maggie gave herself over to the magic of the circus: the clowns tumbling on mats laid over the sawdust, the miniature horse which pranced behind a large white stallion, the trained poodles and pigeons, and the big cats: 'Tigers', she called them, only Packy said 'Lions', as they had no stripes, and the high-wire artist, a young woman in a skimpy pink costume, who had them all breathless, their heads tilted back, as balancing a long pole she made her way miles above them, her shadow huge across the top of the tent.

During the interval Packy bought a bag of popcorn from one of the short dark vendors who circulated among the crowd, offering "circus posters, sweets and souvenirs" in identical tones, like a taped announcement, probably all the English they had. Eating the popcorn, she looked again for Neddy, who no doubt needed a few days to adjust to the circus routine. As she watched a pony carry a child around the ring, she felt again the old ache of the family she and Packy had never had, though she had long ago made her peace there. Besides she could now think of Neddy sharing in the children's delight, once he was sufficiently accustomed to the lights and circus noise. Nor was Maggie any longer worried for his welfare, for the circus animals were clearly looked after—the horses and poodles well-groomed, nothing gaunt or mangy about the big cats or the single camel.

Draining the steaming carrots at the sink, she thought again how ignorance might have remained bliss—had Packy not hailed the circus hand from the Harbour Bar as they made their way from the tent.

"How are you, my friend?" the stocky Bulgarian with a black moustache greeted Packy, including Maggie in the warm sweep of his smile.

"Ask him how Neddy is?" she nudged Packy, who did as he was bid.

"Oh, very good, very good!" the Bulgarian laughed. "The lions, they eats half a donkey already!"

"It's on your head," Maggie told Packy outside the tent, as close as ever she had come to a curse. And it was practically all she said to Packy that evening, feeling still as if her legs had been cut from under her. Except to ask, once Danny had left them home, whether the lions would have eaten Neddy alive?

"No way," Packy said, aware it was cold comfort all the same. "Feeding them live flesh might rekindle their killer instinct," he explained, surprising her again with his knowledge.

As she set the spuds to drain, she saw the magpie back on the wire behind the cottage. Magpies were not that long in the village, and Maggie still took pleasure in the tropical flash of turquoise along their wing. She knew from the radio what a scourge magpies were in Dublin. Driving out songbirds, breaking their eggs even in the nest. But for her, the recently arrived magpies were simply part of the change that underscores life. Changes on every level—even the fridge that kept their dairy milk and store-bought butter where once they had milked and churned. Or the red Zentor Danny drove, twice the size of the grey Fergusons that had once been the only tractors about. Or the TV that now hung in a corner of Biddy's, annoying Packy no end the two nights a week he went down to the pub. Or the physical changes that had overtaken her and Packy over the years, and that would ultimately take them, too, just as they had their own parents.

What's more, the fuss on the radio over the Dublin magpies was rather like the cruelty-to-animals talk you heard in towns—which, for all its good intentions, does not tell the entire story. That life is itself cruel at heart: a lesson you learned early in the country, sobbing over a new-born lamb in a meadow of bluebells, its eyes plucked out by carrion crows. Or crying yourself to sleep over the puppy that had worked its way out of the sack her father had given Liam to throw into the sea, struggling frantically to stay afloat on the sackful of its brothers and sisters as it slowly sank beneath the waves. Never mind the cruelty of humankind that resulted in the bombs across the Border, or the Box for the Starving Black Babies on the Master's desk, or the savage cruelty of the Master himself, who once broke wee Jackie Gara's arm with a single blow. "Sure, didn't he die like a Christian!" her father would have likely laughed at the donkey's fate. Which was how she could forgive—she realised now, hearing Packy at the door—the cruel innocence that had effectively fed her Neddy to the lions.

TRUE RELICS

IT WAS a mention of the Berlin Wall on morning radio that reminded Aiveen of Nelson's Pillar for the first time in donkey's years. A New York entrepreneur it seemed was buying up slabs of the Wall wholesale. Closer to home, Molly was boycotting her breakfast porridge, sweetened with currants instead of sugar.

"Goldilocks never minded currants," Aiveen tried to jolly her four-year-old out of adding salt tears to the already ruined cereal.

"She never had to," Molly sniffed, "cuz the Three Bears hated currants too."

Handy herself with a smart answer at an early age, Aiveen had turned twelve the week the IRA blew Nelson's Pillar to bits along O'Connell Street. The rubble remained for days, as half the Northside took the bus into town to scavenge a souvenir. Her schoolmates brought their scraps into school, cradling them like Relics of the Cross. Some girls boasted theirs were part of the Lord Admiral's hat or sword. Geraldine Sweeney typically claimed to possess an even more personal part of Nelson's equipment.

"Will you take me into town, Mammy?" Aiveen pleaded repeatedly at home. "I'll take you somewheres right enough!" menaced her mother, weeks only out of hospital with her baby brother Leonard. "Why can't you pal with a nice girl like Moira Flynn?" she added, as Geraldine Sweeney came through the front gate.

"Moira's a moan a minute," rejoined Aiveen, hurrying in case her mother asked her to take Leonard along in the pram. What harm if Geraldine's dress was sometimes soiled or her language a little rough, seeing she was a dab hand at rounders and the best on the road at skipping rope? Besides, Moira Flynn had swimming lessons twice a week after school, and talked of little else.

"I'm fed up skipping," Geraldine announced, so Aiveen followed her down to the back field behind the estate. At the far end lay the ruins of the old Belton mansion, where the two girls sometimes spun out their make-believe. "Will ya take this jewel in ransom for the Prince?" Geraldine petitioned that afternoon, proffering a fist-sized lump of granite. The sun-lit flecks of colour in the building stone had always captivated Aiveen, but suddenly another possibility presented itself.

"We met Mrs Flynn, who took me and Geraldine and Moira into town," Aiveen offered, as her mother inspected the outsized nugget of Lord Nelson. Shooting Aiveen a look, she set the stone on the sitting-room mantel. "Yous are not to go into town alone?" she reminded, in case she had it wrong.

"Sure I know that, Mammy," Aiveen decided for once not to ask why. Even if the city centre posed few risks beyond the Groper, a blind old fellah who crossed and recrossed

O'Connell Street on the arm of any female Samaritan yet to encounter his Roman hands.

A month later Auntie Nora had come home from Manchester for a visit. "There you are, love," she handed Aiveen a tiny plastic camera, whose viewfinder offered up images of St Martin de Porres and the Infant of Prague among other icons. In the sitting room Nora nearly spilled her tea when shown the lump of granite.

"You're not serious," she enthused, "a piece of Nelson's Pillar?"

"Tell your Auntie how you got it," her mother urged Aiveen, who was juggling both a lemonade and baby Leonard.

"Why this'll be worth thousands someday!" Nora declared.

"You can take it with you, Auntie!" Aiveen blurted.

"Was that really part of the Pillar," her mother asked once Nora had departed, delighted with her piece of Irish history.

"Oh, yes, Mammy," Aiveen swore, shuttering from the Sacred Heart to St Francis d'Assisi. "Really it was!"

Replacing Molly's porridge with frosted flakes, Aiveen puzzled the sudden urge she felt to confess her lie twenty-five years after the event. Indeed she had confessed to Father Mulcahy at the time, and again to him two years later after she returned from a visit to Manchester, where Auntie Nora had proudly displayed the lump of granite before Uncle Andy and all eight cousins at Sunday dinner. To whom, Aiveen wondered, could she possibly confess now? Father Mulcahy had said nothing about telling the truth at home; besides, her mother had passed away two years ago. While Auntie Nora, whose enthusiasm had abetted her own deception, sat doting in a Manchester nursing home.

"Ideologically sound paperweights," Jack scoffed that evening, when Aiveen mentioned the New York businessman who planned to market his portion of the Berlin Wall piecemeal across America. "The ideal gift for that special capitalist in your life!"

No doubt he would mutter something about Monuments to Colonialism, Aiveen thought, were she to share her story of Nelson's Pillar. Strange how men's minds worked at all.

"Tell me everything you know, Mammy!" Molly had demanded that evening in lieu of a bedtime story. Suspended above the pillow, Aiveen felt a sudden stab of terror in the face of such innocence. "I'll go first, Mammy," relented Molly. "I know my numbers, I know my letters!"

Back in the sitting-room Aiveen glanced at the evening headlines, trumpeting the latest atrocity in the North. A father shot at the Rosary by Loyalist paramilitaries, his only son having been gunned down by the IRA six months before. Such merciless irony, Aiveen decided, summed up the stupidity of it all: the Irish waltzing out their age-old *danse macabre* even as the Berlin Wall came tumbling down. Laying her glasses aside, she uttered a quick prayer for the widowed mother, left behind as the women always are.

To be sure, dynamiting Lord Nelson seemed child's play compared to the assassinations and proxy bombs of recent years. Not to mention the early years, as the severed head of St Oliver Plunkett suddenly hoved into memory. Geraldine had sat beside her on the school outing to Drogheda, whose Cathedral housed that especial relic of Blessed Oliver, whom the Brits had drawn and quartered besides. The head, inside its glass case on a side altar, struck Aiveen as a rare ornament indeed. Too small to be credible, its dry blackened skin and few wisps of grey hair seemed nothing to venerate. "Isn't he the spit of old man Cahill?" Geraldine whispered, and indeed there was a resemblance to the old greengrocer at the end of their road. Blessing herself repeatedly, Aiveen felt neither reverence nor revulsion. Slipping into a newsagent for fruit gums, the two girls barely made it back to the bus on time. Sister Vivian lashed out as usual at Geraldine, but Aiveen stoutly insisted her own need to find a toilet was what delayed them. Set apart on the journey home, Aiveen prayed to Blessed Oliver that Sister Vivian wouldn't tell her mother, who might ban her altogether from playing with Geraldine.

"I'll be up in a minute, Pet," she answered Jack. Having replaced the fireguard, he would next unplug the telly before switching off the back boiler—like a night watchman on the loose. Staring at the embers, Aiveen wondered what had become of Geraldine, who moved with her family to Limerick a year after Lord Nelson's demise. For weeks Aiveen moped under her mother's feet, paying her back for having disapproved of her now lost pal. Whatever had worried her mother about their friendship, anyhow? Doubtless something as silly as her own fears for Molly, like too much sugar at breakfast. Or worrying every time she moved the kitchen clock closer to bedtime that an exhausted Molly might some day learn of her deception. Certainly none of Molly's playmates were cause for concern, beyond Liz Egan whose tantrums Molly occasionally tried on at home for size.

On Holy Week that same year Geraldine and she had set out with three or four younger ones from the road on a forced march. There felt something vaguely religious about the undertaking, yet the pilgrimage only landed them at Dublin Airport. Knackered, the two older girls browbeat Fergus Foley into the fountain beneath a statue of Our Lady outside the airport chapel. Fergus bolted out each time a car passed, but Geraldine pushed him back until he had his bus-fare. The plan was to have a car sent to fetch them, but his father only laughed at Fergus, who had both his dinner and tea taken by the time the weary pilgrims limped into view.

That same summer, however, the two friends outdid themselves on a visit to Geraldine's granny in Harold's Cross, Aiveen having pleaded with her mother for a week to let her go. After the tea with shop-bought cake, an older cousin Mairead led them on a ramble which ended at the Hospice for the Dying. Following Mairead's lead, they tiptoed into a smaller building at the side of the hospital. Only when her eyes adjusted to the dim light, did Aiveen realize they had entered the mortuary. "Take this," Mairead hissed, handing them each a bottle of Holy Water from a table inside the door. Moving quickly down the aisle, they sprinkled the dead of Dublin laid out on either side. Sheeted to the neck, pennies on their eyes, they lay on slabs waiting to be coffined. Some of the faces were awful in death, while others looked merely sleeping. "That one's just dead," Mairead pointed at a young woman, mouth propped shut by a candle stub tucked under her chin.

"Nothing, just watched telly, Mammy," Aiveen replied, when asked what had they got up to in Harold's Cross.

Somehow Aiveen couldn't imagine Geraldine reading at the fire. Or looking in on a daughter asleep before climbing in beside her husband. Surely Geraldine had been too clever to surrender all sense of adventure. Never mind gorgeous enough to have wrangled something more glamorous for herself? Not that glamour's what I'm after, Aiveen thought, turning over again in bed. At least not like at thirteen, sneaking a pint of milk upstairs for her bath à la Cleopatra.

Whatever class of swan she had ultimately proved, she doubted there had ever been an uglier duckling, her smile alone provoking either fright or delight in new babies on the road. "It's the glasses, love," the mothers with prams invariably reassured her, making her cringe. Even now in photographs, those white winged frames, perched on her nose like a gull poised for flight, seemed a cruel joke on her mother's part. The fact they were all you got from the Health Board was beside the point. Already resigned to more ringlets than Medusa, Aiveen had sellotaped her fringe each night, determined to straighten at least that much of her carrot top.

Probably Geraldine's beauty—straight black hair, outsized green eyes, and a mouth like a rosebud—were part of why she had chosen to pal with Ger to begin with. If Aiveen couldn't look like that, at least her best friend could. Equally remarkable was how little her good looks mattered to Geraldine—unlike Moira Flynn who would scan a mud puddle for her own reflection. Geraldine was loyal besides, always insisting Aiveen was herself a smashing beauty. "Maybe in the eyes of the Groper," she replied, making them nearly wet themselves with laughter.

Still, Jack believed her beautiful, and indeed acted upon it, from head to toe, their first years together. They had met at a trade union meeting when An Post where they both worked went out on strike. After signing her up for a picket line, Jack asked her out for a jar. Descended from a long line of shop stewards, he told her of an uncle whose will stipulated his ashes be scattered across the Ukraine.

"There was the usual cock-up of course, and when my aunt went to collect them, she discovered Uncle Eamonn was already at rest under the roses in St Anne's."

"Let's hope they were at least red roses," laughed Aiveen, winning Jack's heart there and then.

Tall and dark, Jack was himself more history buff than union activist. When first she saw his miniature Spanish Civil War battalions, Aiveen laughed aloud, having long suspected men were at heart only boys grown large. Yet boys were more fun at twenty-three than twelve, and Jack had, with his fund of stories and a fondness for fiddle music, gradually won her over. Three years later they married, and two years after that they moved from a rented flat to their own terraced house not far from Aiveen's parents.

The year of Molly's birth however, Aiveen, on maternity leave, suffered a crisis of confidence. It had been a summer of earwigs, thanks to the endless weeks of rain. The bugs unsettled Aiveen, crawling out of their habitual haunts like cut roses, flaunting their sinister tails inside match-boxes and magazines, and one which fell from the cheese grater into a simmering white sauce. That August she and Jack took an old farmhouse for a fortnight in the Wicklow mountains, handy enough for Jack to commute into work. The night Jack stayed in town for a younger brother's twenty-first, Aiveen woke to a muffled whirring from the meadow abutting the back of the house. Peering from the second-storey window, she made out in the heavy fog three pairs of lights, like the eyes on giant insects, threading circles in the night. Terrified, she stared into the ghostly haze that muted both sound and vision, slowly accepting what she saw were not outsized insects, but in fact visitors from outer space. Unable to flee, she began to weep only when the mist lifted sufficiently to reveal three tractors, hurrying to bring in the hay ahead of the rain forecast for dawn.

In fact Aiveen had lived in fear of apparitions ever since seeing *The Song of Bernadette* at age eight. For months after she dreaded being alone. Eyes squeezed shut upon the toilet, she prayed, "Oh, Blessed Virgin, please do not appear before me now, as I simply won't be able for it!" Nor had she been truly able for a vision of space invaders in a Wicklow meadow. Even after Molly's birth that September, Aiveen sensed some part of her had yet to recover from that night.

A child occasions a host of other fears, but Jack and she gradually learned to temper their terror every time Molly ran a fever. For all the joy she brought, a first child rearranges lives overnight, brings the shutters down on late-night sessions and Chinese take-aways. And so by the time Molly turned two, Jack and she had largely settled for whatever the telly offered of a Saturday night. Aiveen to nurse a glass of wine, while Jack diminished a plastic litre of cider so yellow it resembled nothing so much as a bottle of piss. Nor could she deny that year that their love-making often proved perfunctory too.

Then, during Molly's second summer, after Aiveeen had returned part-time to work, a girlfriend offered her a week on Majorca. "My sister was to go," Emer explained in the canteen, "only she's laid-up with a bad back."

"Will the floors be covered with creepy-crawlies?" asked Aiveen, having travelled no farther than Manchester and the Isle of Man. A week later she and Molly were in a hotel on the bay in Palma. As it happened Molly hated the ocean, content to dig in the sand under a hired umbrella. The beach, backed by a strip of high-rise hotels and holiday flats, was crowded with sunbathers of every stripe. Buoyed by the warm salt water, Aiveen chanced swimming out beyond her depth. Emer, single and fancy-free, stayed out until all hours, then slept past noon. The second day Aiveen came upon a neighbourhood of private villas on a hill above the beach. Pushing Molly in her stroller, she returned late each afternoon when the heat had lessened. Nearly asleep now next to Jack, she saw again the indigo convolvulus on the white-washed walls, the sprays of jasmine scenting the narrow lanes.

Stirring sugar into Molly's porridge the next morning, Aiveen thought again of that Majorcan holiday two years before. One night Emer had offered to babysit Molly for a few hours after supper. Keen to watch the sun sink into the sea, Aiveen ordered a glass of wine at the beach restaurant where she and Molly usually lunched. Mario, their waiter, greeted Aiveen like an old friend, sitting down at her table with a beer. Short wiry and mustachioed, he had darted all week among the tables in a flowered shirt and tight mauve trousers, like an exotic Mediterranean butterfly. At lunchtime they chatted about the weather, Molly or her missing husband, to the degree Mario's English permitted. Tonight, however, Mario failed to inquire after Jack. Instead he offered to buy her a nightcap, pronouncing it 'nightcab', at his favourite bar.

Surprising herself, Aiveen accepted. Mario's local boasted more Majorcans than tourists, more Spanish than English songs on the jukebox, but beyond that, it seemed nothing special. Mario himself seemed sweet, but again nothing special. Certainly they found little in common, beyond the possibility of Ireland and Spain sharing, as Mario twice pointed out, the same group in the next World Cup. As they chatted, Aiveen tried not to stare at a bizarrely made-up woman leaning against the end of the bar. "Mother of God!" she exclaimed shortly after, as two lads in overalls carried the mannequin past their table. Declining Mario's suggestion of *un paseo* along the beach, Aiveen let him walk her back to her hotel, where she kissed him goodnight on the cheek, though not before Mario had proposed something beyond a stroll on the sand.

Aiveen had confessed the episode to no one. Certainly not to Emer who was no Geraldine, nothing of that long-ago intimacy between them. In actuality there had been nothing approximating intimacy between her and Mario; yet, whatever about the fleshly gradations of infidelity—which mattered more to men than to women she suspected, more to Jack than to her—in her heart she had felt unfaithful for a moment, and where, if not in the heart, does fidelity reside?

She felt guilty for a few weeks following her return to Dublin, troubled by the triteness of a holiday fling that in fact had never flung. As transgressions go, the incident felt far greater than the sum of its parts, outweighing any lie she had ever told, even the business of Nelson's Pillar. Why she had even entertained the notion, however, was less of a mystery. To be courted again, to be made feel desirable still, was a strong hand to entirely pass up. However, she had done little, done well to call it a night when she had, and by autumn had forgiven herself whatever trespass.

Still, that was more absolution than she had ever granted herself over the Lord Nelson affair. Or so she decided after breakfast, bundling Molly into her coat for school. Which might explain her search that morning for a scrap of paper with an address for Geraldine's family in Limerick. Or why she found herself wondering which of her eight cousins had inherited that piece of granite.

"Sausages," said Molly at lunch time.

"I asked what you did today," Aiveen laughed, "not what you wanted to eat?"

"Sausages," insisted Molly. "One of us is the cook, and the rest of us jump around 'til the pan's too hot, then we hop out and run away for cook to chase."

"I don't remember playing that in school?"

"How could you, Mammy?" laughed Molly. "I made it up!"

Telling Jack that night, she sensed beyond her pride in Molly's cleverness a wish that her daughter might prove better able for it all. Certainly Aiveen had never dreamed up a schoolyard game, something far more likely of Geraldine. As it was, Molly had blossomed ever since the past summer in Donegal. At first Jack had proposed a sun holiday, until Aiveen allowed she had seen enough of Spain. So they settled on

Donegal, despite her fear of the IRA activity that was occasionally reported along its border with Derry. Choosing instead the southwestern coast, they hired a holiday house in a small village west of Killybegs. Luck was with them, as the sun shone the entire fortnight. "Sure, we've the Mediterranean here at home!" joked Mrs Gillespie, who hired out the new chalet in its meadow of buttercups and rushes. "Aren't you a great gissy!" she fussed over Molly, offering a boiled sweet from her apron pocket whenever they passed her gate en route to the strand.

This summer Molly charged straight into the ocean, which to Aiveen felt ten times colder than Majorca. When Molly tired of sand castles, they would leave Jack napping under a newspaper and climb beyond the dunes to the warren alive with rabbits, to sit quietly at the bottom of a hollow riddled with rabbit holes, Aiveen dozing in its sun trap, until a rabbit would poke out its head to Molly's utter delight. On the road back, Molly imagined herself a mountain goat, picking her way along the stone ditches, as Aiveen gathered armfuls of dog daisies and Queen Anne's lace.

"Would we go back to Donegal this summer?" Jack asked that evening as if reading her thoughts.

"I'll ring Mrs Gillespie in the morning," Aiveen replied. If Donegal had given Molly a leg up on life, it had also helped Jack and her breach the wall of routine between them. Even Jack's passion for the past had taken on life there, as he led them some distance to a sea cave where Bonnie Prince Charles was said to have hidden from English soldiers.

"I should've known it was your bloomin' history," Aiveen teased the afternoon they left Mrs Gillespie in charge of Molly, "not a holiday that brought us here." Climbing up the hill at the far end of the strand, they struck out north in search of an isolated glen where, legend had it, Charles had kept his rendezvous with a French sailing ship. They passed a few men bagging turf, turning occasionally to admire the village scattered out below, the distant curve of a further headland cradling the sea to the south, dark clouds trailing mare's tails over mountains to the east. To their left, out to sea, the western sky was entirely clear, the sun a red ball sinking toward the horizon.

"Did you ever see such colours?" Aiveen asked as the trail descended sufficiently to block out the vista behind. Turning their sights inland, they drank in the chartreuse patches of grass, the heather in blossom like pools of purple, the scattered bog banks a vibrant brown. Shortly after Aiveen herself came in colours, eyes closed, astride Jack in a small hollow off the path. Afterwards, her head on his chest, she listened to the whine of a single midge, birdsong, a sheep bleating, the mutter of a distant tractor at the turf.

"Do you think we'll find that hidden glen this summer?" she straight-faced Jack that evening as he switched off the back boiler.

"Why not get a head-start tonight," he laughed, "if you're not forever coming up to bed?"

"According to Mrs Gillespie," he said as she unbuttoned his shirt, "there's a remnant of Charles' shaving towel in the village yet."

"Shroud of Turin, how are ye?" Aiveen rejoined, loath to let on how the idea of the Pretender once in those hills had taken her fancy too.

"There's Germans who wanted July," explained Mrs Gillespie next morning over the phone, "but I'll only give them the first fortnight. Germans always leave a place cleaner than they find it," she laughed, "so yous can come up the same day they leave."

Putting down the phone, Aiveen suddenly remembered the small bottle in the kitchen press at the chalet the previous summer. "Fizzy orange, Mammy!" Molly had crowed, recognizing the label. "That's not orange, Pet," Aiveen sniffed its clear contents. Then, compulsive cleaner that she was, she emptied it down the sink, only to spy too late the 'Holy Water' pencilled on the label. Unnerved, she had quickly refilled it from the kitchen tap and replaced it in the press.

Now, smiling in her own kitchen, Aiveen saw it as all of a piece: the phony Pillar fragment, the gift-sized bits of the Berlin Wall, the unblessed Holy Water, even the not-to-be-believed noggin of Blessed Oliver. If Auntie Nora had been thrilled with a lump of old granite, taking it on faith, would the next holiday crowd at the chalet be any less blessed by bottled water? Might not misplaced belief prove every bit as efficacious as a bouquet placed before the real McCoy?

Preparing a sandwich for Molly's lunch, she recalled Jack's delight in a curved length of heavy timber he found on the strand in Donegal, believing it the rib of a sailing ship beached there a century before. And if they reached that distant glen this summer, might not they find a deserted cottage there? Encircled by waist-high nettles, thatch tumbling in, key still on the latch. If so, from its kitchen dresser she might claim a small delft jug, chipped at the spout and patterned with a single wild rose. And if not, she would gladly settle for her memories—of Geraldine skipping rope or Molly's first steps—relics as true as any fragments of oak or stone.

COINS

IT WAS JACK who found them, lying by his meadow gate where Campbell had dumped the three hundredweight of phosphates and potassium. Bag manure as Jack calls it. He saw a dull gleam, picked one up, spied another, and a third. The coins were no ways hidden, lying on the grassy verge. It was a wonder Campbell hadn't seen them, if they were there when he made delivery.

A greater wonder had Campbell dropped them, someone jests in the pub where Jack shows the coins that evening. Last winter when the jackpot hit three hundred, the story went that Campbell and wife showed up for the first time in memory at the church hall, each of them buying a book of numbers. When a small widow with a large family shouted "Bingo!", Campbell strode out in disgust.

There is no truth to the tale of the shopkeeper at the church hall. Nor is it necessarily true that he is any more tight-fisted than his neighbour. Campbell surely sees it otherwise. "Come on now! There're no pockets in a shroud," he coaxes elderly customers anyways slow to pay for a bag of sheep nuts, a cylinder of bottled gas. "Time enough," Jack counters, observing Rome wasn't burnt in a day.

The words embossed on the specie make no cents or pence to Jack who thought them German. A reasonable assumption, as mostly Germans come in summer now to marvel at the mountains and sea. They hardly seem to mind the rain, in fair weather seat themselves outside the crossroads pub in their *lederhosen*. To look or listen you might easily think it a Bavarian village. Like Americans the Germans speak loudly, festooned in photographic gear. But Yanks you know by their shirt pockets: bulging with biros and candy bars.

The design on the currency is as foreign. What resembles a palm tree is possibly a windmill. Or crow's nest. Nothing so simple as salmon, a harp, or royalty from a neighbouring isle. Not to date a story before its time, let me merely say that the coins number three consecutive years of the previous decade. "French," I inform Jack when he shows me them the next day. From across deep water, I've seen something of the world, and Jack takes my word. Francs, ten-franc pieces. "Worth over a pound each," I add, after some rapid mental maths.

"You've no French, Jack," I kid him. "Give me them to flog to the first Jacques or Jean I meet, and we'll split fifty-fifty."

"Hugh Doyle would be the man for the job," says Jack, pocketing the coins. Every time he finds me with a book, Jack speaks of Hugh Doyle, a clever man who taught University, spoke six or seven tongues. Balmy from too many brains, he came to live with his nephew here in the townland. Hugh Doyle would call into Jack for a chat, sit by the fire and doodle with a pencil on the white-washed wall.

"Would you not mark the kitchen, Hugh?"

"Well, I won't!" and he would put away his pencil. A few minutes later he would forget himself, and take it out again.

Then, as now, French trawlers fished these coastal waters. One day the guards arrested some of a crew who had come in too near with a dory after lobster. The guards were escorting the French lads from the pier when Hugh Doyle came down the lane. A lively conversation followed in French at the meadow gate, the two police standing by like eejits.

"Three coins in a fountain," I tell Jack who has not seen the film. And I have but a few words to the song, the remainder lost somewhere in the heart of Rome. *The Return of Frank James* he greatly enjoyed, paying three separate admissions. I tell him of the Trevi Fountain regardless. "If you don't travel, you know nothing," Jack translates from his native tongue, echoing the old man up the north side of the village who gave him that advice as a child. Several sandwiches short of a picnic, the old man never left home himself. Still, you wouldn't know where he hadn't wandered in that kind of mental haze. Travelling light, I suppose. That somebody was never seven miles from a cow's tail is as contemptuous as Jack gets. He has roved farther afield himself, but I am never able to get out of him just where or when.

I don't get the coins for a while either, though I make the odd attempt to cadge them. I find it curious though that Jack takes them from a pocket of his trousers when I mention them another evening. We are seated by the warren, watching the rabbits roll in the sand.

"They'll bring you bad luck," I laugh.

"You've no luck yourself," Jack rejoins. "I wouldn't like to be the man who saw two strange birds, birds never before seen here." He is serious, too.

I first saw the birds around the time he found the coins. There were two of them in it, larger than crows, something vaguely unbalanced about their flight. Black head and wings, their back and tail a uniform brown. "They're not pulling together," Jack observes when I describe how rooks from the rectory orchard chased them over the bay.

"I wish you would see them," I say. "To help identify them," I explain. But Jack, frowning, shakes his head in a manner that brings the Middle Ages to mind.

Jack worries about me, and sometimes that makes two of us. He believes that I spend too much time alone inside. Of an age with my father, he is a good neighbour who often drops by for a chat. "You should marry," he counsels. "A small widow with a large family," who would bring a substantial stipend from the state as well. An elderly woman with a long lane and a hard cough. Or, better yet, a schoolteacher with a public house. "She would be away days," he points out, "leaving her man the premises." He is dead set against marrying a nurse.

When Jack displays the coins again one evening at the pub, the penny drops, so to speak. Finally it dawns on me that he is in fact carrying them for luck. Somebody drops one of the trio on the flagstone floor, the test of its worth how sharply it rings out. Another villager, retrieving the coin, tries it between his teeth. Someone else recalls the priest, now dead, who rued a silent collection, as coppers tossed onto the church-door table do not sing out as silver does. "You could hear him a mile off" as was said of Judas, once he had his money made.

The party who bit the money remembered a visitor from the Bronx, when it was still customary to make an offering as the remains arrived for a funeral Mass. The amount and donor's name were read off as you entered the chapel. A mistaken case of when in Rome, the Yank, one of those blokes always mad for an auction, begins to bid himself. Throws down five dollars, hollers out his name.

It is hardly surprising Jack might consider the coins enchanted, as I've heard from him and others the story of a fairy shilling in this very parish. A man out walking one evening came upon a strange woman heavily burdened with a basket. He offers to carry it over the road, and she assents. It feels to him to weigh next to nothing, but he passes no remarks. The woman turns off at a neighbour's lane, saying she has a sick call there. "Do you ever take a drink?" she asks your man. "Aye, I do, sometimes, at a fair or the like," he allows. "Well, then, maybe you'll drink my health with this," says she, and gives him a shilling. He watches her go up the lane, sees her in the light from the cottage as the door opens to admit her.

Curious, he calls down to his neighbour the next day, but the man of the house swears nobody called in the previous evening. Nor was there anybody ill about the place. Your man finds it a bit odd, but proceeds to the shop where he buys a bottle of stout and some plug tobacco with the coin. On the way home he discovers the shilling among the few coppers in his pocket.

No matter how often he spends the coin then, it always returns to him. In the end he becomes troubled by it, the ready availability of drink if nothing else. Some say he flung the coin into the sea from a height, only to find it again in his trousers. One day he mentions it to the priest whom he meets along the road. "Show me it," the priest demands, and when the man brings out his hand, the shilling is gone. Rendered unto Caesar, whatever about the Fairy Host.

"That's Gospel," Jack and the others always conclude, a claim by no means made for every story told. What is remarkable, for me, is knowing the very bend in the road, the ill neighbour's house, or the large white rock that figures in another tale. The shilling man met the strange woman in the townland where Jack and I reside and you could roughly date the event as well. His daughter I sometimes visit, a woman of nearly ninety. As happens, our fathers died both on the same Feast Day, in somewhat similar and unusual circumstances. The shilling man fell on the hill road to chapel here, my father between the Gospel and Offertory in a faraway land. "Anything strange?"—a common greeting in this locality— encourages my sometimes notion that no such thing exists as an idle phrase.

Beyond that I make no claims. To assiduously question any belief is to end up arguing religion, a dangerous undertaking on this or any island. Last summer my neighbour Jesse visited Mallorca with his brother. They had little money, but Jesse plays the guitar, the brother a mandolin, and both have lovely voices. One afternoon they find themselves playing music in a dusty mountainy village. No doubt they are a remarkable sight to the locals, their fair hair bleached by the sun that has burned them a dark brown, clad only in white shorts and leather sandals. Add to that their music, the songs sung in a strange tongue, and you can easily imagine the scene. The villagers are enchanted, litres of wine appear, bottles of cognac follow. In a corner of the *bodega* sits an old man with one leg. "Angels of God," he intones, "Angels of God," marvelling at his vision. Perhaps he insists too much upon it, for an equally old man with one arm takes exception. Amid the violence that follows, the two lads take wing. Whatever about Heaven, their haven seemingly lies somewhere else.

Sometimes Jack and I sit on a ditch which is the word for a stone wall here. Oats elsewhere are corn in this corner. What I know as a barrel Jack calls a bottle, and sheep nuts are not what they sound. One afternoon two visitors from the capital stop to chat. They want directions, but I am as loath to give these as I am to offer advice. They are young women on holiday, and we talk of the difference between urban and rural life. One is a schoolteacher, the other a civil servant. Both are called Mary. Jack is a small farmer, I suppose, and I do a bit of writing, though the idea that you are how you earn has not yet gained currency here. Jack informs them they can stop with me, that I live alone, and there are these empty rooms. I ask them in for tea, and Jesse who is English and lives up the lane calls down. Once he leaves, the schoolteacher asks, "Are there any Irish here at all?" "Yourselves and Jack," I offer, thinking her rather young to own much property, whatever about a pub.

Another day Jesse and I meet two hikers along the road. One of them is a French lass with a vast cloud of hair, distant eyes, sunbrown face, her slight form lost in the billows of a grandfather shirt. She asks directions to the hostel, and this time I make an exception, though her shelter lies the other side of the hill from my empty rooms. I remark upon her eyes to Jesse as we carry on. He nods, tells of a waitress in a café on another island where he was on holiday years ago. As business was slow she joined his party, sat down to talk for a while. Jesse sees her face still, dreams of her yet.

That evening I decide to ask Jack again for the coins, thinking they would give Mademoiselle and I something to discuss, should we meet again. To speak *francly*, as it were, trusting they won't disappear if I chance to show her them. Somehow I believe her a nurse, though maybe it's just the idea of that brown skin against a uniform white. Was the strange woman making the sick call years back by any chance an Angel of Mercy also?

"I may as well give you them," Jack says. "I've had no luck since." I think to inquire how many fishermen were arrested long ago. Three he tells me. "The Three Musketeers," Jack laughs. There is a new film version of that story also I inform him.

As I pocket the thirty francs, I suddenly recall a curious coin that has passed already through my hands. It was in a small seaside town the other side of the island, a drink with friends. One of the party is a lad named Jules, and the two of us are somewhat taken with a girl called Lisa. My round, I'm standing at the bar to order. "A penny for your thoughts," Lisa offers Jules, as if to call his bluff. With her words I spy a bright copper at my feet. "Money on the floor," my sister used to sing, skipping rope. "Won't you pick it up, pick it up, money on the floor."

"Pay up," I tell Lisa, tossing it over, only it glances off our table to roll across the room. Jules points out a tall girl in blue jumper and blue jeans, but when I make inquiries, she shrugs her slender shoulders. His father's business was what Jules had in mind, so we depart upon downing our drink. Leaving, I meet the lass in blue by the door where she lays a hand upon my arm. In a rush of embarrassment she owns up to her dissembling.

"Piss off," I inform Jules who attempts to cut in, apposite idiom for what is to follow.

"Do you have it yet?" I ask.

"I'm sorry, I haven't. I used it in the loo."

"You spent a penny!" I crow with delight. Her tiny dance of delight suggests she too feels we've again coined the phrase, the words as freshly minted as any copper.

"I need to see a man about a donkey," was how my father always excused himself. If he never met the donkey man, someone undoubtedly somewhere did, just as someone else will do so again. Percy to be pointed at the porcelain, a tear shed for the nation once again. Dry-eyed I follow Jules through the door.

In the car-park Lisa says that you don't have to pay for the jacks in that pub. Not usually literal-minded, she is perhaps a tiny bit jealous. "Two pints and I'm anybody's!" says Jules, and I'm much the same way. "Three hearts in the fountain," chants Jack when he gets tight. "Which one will the fountain bless?"

"Is there anything to these stories?" folk sometimes ask. Convenient fictions is as much as I care to hazard. Besides, you would have only my word for it, less than a bank manager would accept, leery of any currency that fluctuates so. Coinage like *Liberté* and her two sisters who masquerade round the rim of my French money like three more musketeers. Not entirely a specious belief, I feel, or is it that I'm too long on this island, where at least half the lies they tell you prove untrue?

In the newspaper I read of another country where you are likewise left in a remote corner, required to observe the rules of your banning there. Here winters are worse than summers, when the village fills up with other strangers. They are easy to identify in yellow gumboots, whereas the natives are all in black. Lisa, well-travelled herself, argues there are only states of mind, no statute of limitations on their books at all. Not wholly persuaded, I tell her of a tramp I saw as a child in the Trevi Fountain an hour before dawn. Trousers rolled to the knee, he fished his luck in the unlit waters. "It's free to get in, but you pay to get out," observed my father as the *Carabinieri* hauled the poor man away. That he chose the darkest hour is Lisa's rejoinder. Or, when in Rome, put up with it? It seems the old man up the north side spent his last years shouting "Bingo! Bingo!" as he shuffled about the cottage. "Damn the numbers!" he would wail when he was not winning.

"Marks, my word!" laughs Campbell who does a great trade in black pudding with the Germans. *Free Answers to Your Questions* a sign in his shop informs us. *This Offer Applies Especially in Summer Months.* "Which road leads out of here?" I intend to query when the time is ripe. "When you don't know where you're headed," said my father, "any road will take you there." On my way across the island to see Lisa, I meet a lad beside the highway, holding a small sign lettered *ROME*. "Isn't it all the one road leading there?" he expounds, offering me half a sandwich.

"No sign of those foreign birds since?" asks Jesse whose London argot throws me from time to time. To date I've not seen either pair again, though I'm not without hope. Jack worries always that I'm headed the way of Hugh Doyle. I haven't the brains for the job, I assure him. Moreover I have an eye out for the writing on the wall.

Meantime the French coins are somewhere in these three rooms, unless they fell out a hole in my pocket. Whatever about fishing limits, you do not so easily flout the law of eternal return. Jesse suggests I have the I-Ching speak with a Gallic accent in this Gaelic setting. Myself, I am as happy to be rid of them, for you make your own luck, surely? Nor do I care to be always prepared to pay my way out. I carry nothing in my shirt pockets at any rate; to travel light like your woman with the basket.

Besides, I had begun to worry that money might be the root of all language, as if in every tale told the words would want to ring true. "Make every word count!" they cautioned at school, setting us to write of our summer holidays. "They are all of them good days," Jack reminded me when I especially enthused over one sunlit afternoon not long ago. Perhaps I am struggling yet with that assignment, stranded in this village on holidays of obligation as they are known at home? *Behold the Bread of Angels!* advises a banner in the village on the Feast Day my father died.

Its legend prompted Jack to tell of his grandfather who lived to a great age. Badly doting, he shared a bed with his grandson three years old. One night a cake of bread is left to cool on the kitchen table. Waiting his chance, Jack brings it to bed, only to lose it beneath the blankets. His grandfather, finding the bread, falls to it. When Jack snatches the loaf back, the old man begins to roar. "Where's the scone that God give me," he sobs himself to sleep.

"Do you want your pennies from Heaven?" I inquire of Jack.

"Hang onto them," he says. "Should you ever be in that country again." All the same I cod him that I am writing an account of his funny money, only I've set it in the heart of Rome. "Don't bring me into it," he cautions. "I don't want to pay income tax."

"I won't, Jack," I assure him. If ever I get down to it, I'll bring him back as Frank or Jesse James. Travelling, like you and I, under assumed names in the on-going story. Money is truly a many-splendoured thing.

FINDERS, KEEPERS

NORA SPOONED the treacle into the pan of warm milk, stirring until it turned a uniform brown. Pouring the liquid into the flour, she worked the dough with her hands, adding the currants last. The scone shaped, she floured it lightly, then cut a cross on top. While her Tom was as fond of treacle bread as Sean, Nora seldom made it now unless Sean was home on a visit. This evening Sean would return from Africa forever, but Nora was in no ways certain Tom would break bread at the same table with their elder son.

It was six months since Sean had written of his intention to leave the priesthood—to marry an American girl he had met in Ghana. He added his superiors had asked him to defer any decision until autumn, conditions which he readily accepted. Staggered by the news, his father had since scarcely even spoken of Sean. While she hoped Tom would come round, Nora had seen no signs of any change of heart. To judge by her husband, it was as if their elder son were dead and buried.

The six months, if not easy, passed quickly. Then, yesterday, a telegram had come from Sean who was flying into Dublin today. The news had taken them unawares, but it was likely just as well. If not finesse, Sean would at least force his father's hand. Tom, true to form, said nothing when the telegram arrived. It was Nora who rang Donal, their youngest, to collect Sean at Dublin Airport. Ruing such short notice, she had time only to air the boys' bedroom, buy a joint of meat and bake the treacle bread.

On his last visit Nora had baked a plain soda scone as well. Seated on the sofa before the low table in the parlour, Sean had taken the scone, blessed it, and handed it out as Holy Eucharist. All without benefit of surplice, without any linen on the ad hoc altar. The congregation was mostly a handful of older neighbours, the morning lovely, the sun through the net curtains polishing the wooden rhino on the window ledge. Over the fireplace hung the wooden heads, a knife and scabbard, carved wooden masks—a West African hearth in the heart of Ireland.

Nora would remember forever how Donal had nudged Sean afterwards, pointing to a crust at their feet. Grinning, Sean retrieved and swallowed it, reminding her how he used to court her displeasure by offering grace whenever Tom was late for tea. "Holy Mary, Mother of God, say a prayer for the man in the bog."

Afterwards Nora heard how it had been the nicest Mass her neighbours had ever attended, belying her initial apprehension. "Our Lord's first Eucharist was only a supper," Sean had reminded her. "And we rarely use an altar cloth in Ghana, where the long-life altar wine works like battery acid if you spill a drop."

"Besides, you worry too much about the neighbours."

"Go on, you," Nora said. Nor did she give in to the neighbours either—not even in the early days. Even now she could recall that first night in Lahan, peering out as the hackney drew up to the crossroads, where what looked like a hundred eyes peered back at her from out of the dark.

"What's that shining?" she asked her husband of one week, thinking it some kind of phosphorescence in the fields.

"Goats," said the bridegroom and so they were. At least sixty goats bedded down for the night, more goats than Nora had ever seen in Sligo. Without doubt Tom's Tipperary seemed a queer place altogether. The village houses all papered with crazy patterns: geometric shapes, diamonds and intricate lattice-work. Kitchen floors, including Nelly's, her mother-in-law, that boasted large black and white linoleum squares— reminding Nora of a painting of a Dutch interior her mother had cut out of a magazine. Such foreign walls and floors only further fed the feeling she was astray in a maze, newly married in a strange land.

And it seemed easily a hundred eyes were on her, day and night. "You can be sure they are!" laughed Ita Burke when Nora first confessed her paranoia. Her next-door neighbour, Ita quickly proved a saint, her saviour, their friendship easing Nora into village life. Close as they would grow, two women never looked less alike: Ita short, dark and lively to Nora's larger, fair, placid self. Already two years wed when Nora landed in Lahan, Ita gave birth the following year to her only child, Colum, a fortnight before Nora had Sean. "It wouldn't do to be outdone by the likes of you," she informed Nora who visited her in hospital.

Cradlemates, the two lads proved the mortar between their mothers. Pram-mates, playmates, schoolmates, together they headed their class. The priest in charge of the school naturally encouraged the brightest boys—and at seventeen Sean and Colum left together for the seminary. Four years later, Colum bailed out, a week before their ordination. Nora had baked her best friend's son a cake for the occasion, which Colum hid beneath his bed for a week until he had it eaten. When three years later Sean wrote from Africa of his decision, Nora confided at once in Ita, certain of her audience.

"We'll tell nobody," Tom declared that first night, in the event Sean might change his mind. Intending to tell Ita only, Nora sensed the neighbours were not incidental to Tom. Should his pride be anyways wounded, he was after all from Lahan—where Nora would forever remain an outsider.

Still his intransigence puzzled her. A large slow man, slow to anger, Tom was in most things more reasonable than not. Whenever he entered the house when the children were young, he would invariably glance up at the meter. Were the dial spinning, he would set off to mildly reprimand whoever had left whatever lights on. Far more of himself in this routine than in the shunning of his elder son.

What's more, neither of them had ever made a public display over Our Son, the Priest. Nothing akin to the banner—*Another Soldier for Christ*—that Mrs Hartnett hung above her door the day her Matt was ordained. "It sounds more marching than holy orders for young Hartnett," Tom observed that evening. While never rabid on the subject, Tom occasionally gave out about the clergy. "You used to shake as a child, whenever you saw a guard or priest. And the Missions were worst, the entire village turned out like at a circus." What Tom described, Nora knew from her own Sligo. The Mission generally comprising a pair of priests, one loud, one soft.

Together they played their congregation like a fish on a line: one padre hauling hard, the other paying out a bit of slack. As one preached, the other heard Confession, Benediction and Rosary following. Nor was it unheard of for the talk of damnation to send some poor sinner home to suicide. During the Mission, green stalls like those at a sheep fair lined the street outside the church, offering scapulars and crucifixes in lieu of wellington boots and second-hand trousers. Nothing so colourful as the fair-day trader who used to query: "Show me the man who won't cover the hole in his arse for eight bob?"

"At least with John the XXIII the bulldozing was done," Tom credited his favourite Pontiff with having made the priests get out and mix. Not until Vatican II had he seen his first Bishop off the altar, chatting with two merchants in Tipperary Town. A priest was no bother in his place, per Tom, which ruled out the football pitch where the parish curate reffed Sunday afternoons. "It's not right, that," Tom asserted, prompting Sean at fifteen to add you never saw the Lahan club captain togged out and distributing Communion at the rail.

That day Nora had silenced them both. Only to puzzle two years later that such a father should see such a son find a vocation. What made more sense was Sean's choice of the White Fathers—a missionary order—little given to large Ford Escorts with golf clubs in the boot.

Once ordained, Sean was sent to Ghana, where his letters home told of another world. Teaching school, he was ministering to minds as well as souls, bemused by his students' essays. "Ghanaians not only christen themselves with random English words," he wrote, "but they change them at a whim. Prudence who submits a paper on Friday is likely to be

Comfort the following Monday." Another letter told of card games at night:

As we play, mangoes fall onto the tin roof. Our game ends when four have fallen. We find them in the dark, then walk out into the sea and sit in the water to our necks while we eat the fruit. It's easier to see how Your Man provides in this climate. May He keep you and Father well...

Home on holidays, Sean showed them a snapshot of an elephant, its trunk like a question mark. "It charged as I took this," he explained. "I made for a grass hut fifty yards behind me. Two natives stood either side the door, hands outstretched, going 'Welcome, welcome!' as I shot past."

"It didn't follow?"

"Apparently they bluff a lot."

It was this visit Sean gave Tom the ring for his birthday. A small, square-cut sapphire, set in a simple band of gold.

"You've no funds for this," protested his father.

"Who said I paid for it?"

"You stole it, then?"

"That would be telling," Sean said, telling instead how a sixth-century Papal Bull directed every Cardinal to wear a sapphire. "A sapphire also enabled a sorcerer to hear voices prophesying."

"Nothing wrong in hearing voices," Tom said, trying on the ring, "provided you don't answer them."

"Sapphires were also considered an aid to chastity."

"Small wonder the Pope prescribed it for his Cardinals, so," his father smiled.

"Thomas," Nora cautioned.

"Mind he doesn't grow too fond of it?" Sean laughed.

"That's enough from the pair of you," his mother declared.

"Did you ever know a priest to be such a penance," Tom placed the photograph of the elephant beside his chair. And not many callers escaped hearing of the mangoes on the roof either.

As Nora took the scone from the oven, the doorbell rang, signalling the post. Outside a gale was blowing, rain belting down—likely to fall now from Hallowe'en to Easter. Hoping for a letter from Maggie, Nora found only a bill from the ESB. Their middle child, Maggie had gone up to Dublin three years before to work in the bank. Before long she was doing a line with a co-worker from Cork, a nice lad whom Maggie brought home in July. Unlike Sean's letter, the news of their engagement that visit had surprised neither Nora nor Tom.

The ESB bill came as no surprise either—though the sum was no less outrageous for that, as only Tom and herself were left now to leave on any lights. Setting it aside, Nora faced once again toward the evening, sensing amid her misgivings a potential relief, like visiting the dentist with a septic tooth. Only here the abscess had festered for half a year, in which Nora twice lit the fire with a page from the *Tipperary Star* which promised "A Priest in Your Family for Only £1 a Week!" to any reader willing to sponsor one of many qualified but impoverished Peruvian seminarians. Nora marvelling, as she struck the match, that Tom, for all his irreverence, should prove the one to suffer most over their Sean's lost vocation.

The sitting-room fire laid, Nora went up to clean the bathroom. In August they had installed an indoor toilet, its construction only further disordering their lives. Despairing at the plaster and sawdust tracked through the house, Nora consoled herself with the prospect of no longer trudging winters through the garden to the toilet at the back.

The Sunday after the workmen left, Tom's mother Nelly, two doors down, died in her sleep. Plagued by bronchitis and badly doting, Nelly had refused to the last to come down to them. Twice that summer she had paced the street outside her door, rigged out in a black hat and black gloves for Sean's funeral. As if she somehow sensed, midst her confusion, something amiss between her son and her favourite grandson. "Do you walk out over the hills?" she would ask Sean home on holiday—Ghana in her mind no different to Tipperary. "I'm awaiting the remains from Africa!" she remonstrated with Nora—who twice enlisted Father Cullen to cajole the old woman indoors.

That same Sunday Nora had coaxed Tom out for a walk after Mass. They took the lane from the church to the river, passing fields either side strewn with meadowsweet. As they neared the old oak by Tucker's Gate, they saw some distance ahead of them a dark form leave a small outbuilding and cross the lane. The sound of several voices hung lightly for a moment on the heavy August air.

"What kind of confab have we here?" wondered Nora aloud. Passing the shed, they saw no sign of life within it or the field opposite. "We brushed it from our eyes," Nora told Ita that night, "only to come home and find the old woman dead."

They buried Nelly two days later, Donal and Maggie coming down from Dublin for the funeral. There was no question of Sean attending, as he lived a two-day trek from a plane to London, never mind the thirty-six hours it took a telegram to track him down.

It was at the churchyard Tom lost the ring. Or so he thought, recalling how one of his sisters had admired it there. Over the next weeks he returned repeatedly to the grave. "To tend the flowers," he told Nora, who sensed that was only part of it. That he was looking for the ring heartened her, as had the fact he had not taken it off after Sean's letter landed.

"You can't just bury the living!" she wanted to tell Tom each time he went out. "Were I Ghanaian," she informed Ita, "I'd name myself either Patience or Despair."

The Gospel a week after Nelly's death was on the Prodigal Son. And, in the event Luke had failed to spell it out for Tom, Father Cullen surely hammered it home, explaining how the father's clemency was only an emblem of divine mercy. "After forgiving his wayward child," he read aloud, "he slipped a ring onto his son's hand."

As she shifted on the unforgiving pew, Nora considered how heretofore their Donal had played the prodigal more than Sean. Eternally grateful neither son was given to drink, Nora had come into the kitchen a few years back to find Donal before the range.

"What are you at, putting that nasty weed into my oven?"

"Trying to dry it, Mammy."

"Would you not think of hanging it in the sun?"

"Sure, I never thought of that Mammy," Donal smiled, as if it were the first clever idea she ever had. A fortnight later she found him sorting leaves from stems on a newspaper spread over the kitchen table.

"What do you do with that now?"

"I smoke it."

"But I thought you didn't smoke tobacco?"

"I don't smoke tobacco," replied her youngest. "I smoke this."

Then, remembering she used to smoke, he offered her some of the strange leaves.

"Go on away out of that now," Nora said. "It'd only make a reel in my head!" And that was all she said. That Sunday there was an article in the paper which suggested Donal was on the road to ruin, but Nora trusted her sons farther than that.

Like Maggie, Donal went up to Dublin, where he met a girl from Clare. After he and Detta set up housekeeping together, Donal took pains to keep the arrangement from home. Indeed Nora had thought Tom unawares, until a visit home when Donal likewise mentioned marriage.

"What's your hurry?" his father responded, revealing a pliancy that surprised both son and wife. Settling on a September wedding, Donal and Detta went to Spain in May, which prompted Tom to inform Ita, "Nowadays they have the honeymoon ahead of the wedding." The wedding came off in September all the same, and Donal had settled down in fine fashion.

Nora had the fatted calf in the oven by the time Ita called in. "We'll have a cup of tea so," Nora declared, not having stopped all day.

"I brought you this," Ita said, laying a barmbrack on the table. "I knew you'd hardly have time for Hallowe'en and a homecoming both."

"Wednesday is Hallowe'en, right enough," Nora said. "Did you put a ring in it?" she laughed, remembering how Ita's Colum had once broken a tooth on a slice of brack.

"Do you believe Father Cullen's having a concert on Wednesday?"

"On the Night of the Dead!" Ita replied. "Will they do the fifteen decades of the Rosary first?"

"You'd be wakened at midnight," Nora reminisced, "no ways fit to pray."

"The older ones would have sat up to tend the fire."

"You'd have a good fire anyways," Nora agreed.

"Sure, you'd want to die soon—to die a Catholic," Ita smiled, telling how she had recently discovered 'Bon Voyage' cards stocked under 'Vocations & Ordinations' at Eason's in Tip Town.

Cutting two slices off the barmbrack, Nora voiced her misgivings over the evening's reunion. If Ita's reassurance did little, at least Nora had got to speak straight from the heart in a way she seldom managed with Tom. Though later, seated alone, awaiting her sons and husband, Nora finally spoke out to him.

"Do you not know you need to let go, Tom? Hadn't I to leave Sligo and my family both. And didn't I see Sean go to

Africa and, likely enough, America next. You laugh about the Church—Mammy's Priests and so on—but it's you who tell those stories of Ghana, you who are holding on. Can you not see you have to let go, else you risk losing him forever?"

Her speak finished, Nora moved to tidy the tea things, wiping her eyes as she rose. Yet two hours later, as she set the joint before her husband, it was as if somehow he had heard her out. The reunion had begun awkwardly enough—Donal arriving with Sean to find Tom in his habitual chair, arms crossed. He rose however to shake hands with both sons. After a bit of strained chat about the flight from Africa, Sean had taken a set of Rosary beads from his jacket pocket. Fashioned from rosewood, they were a Maher family treasure, Tom's gift to Sean upon his ordination.

"Do you want these back now?" his son asked, voice soft with the challenge.

Nora held her breath until Tom waved his own hand. "Hang onto them so. You'll likely be a father of another sort soon enough."

And so, when the lights went during the meal, Nora was in no ways put out. "Sure the bill came only this morning," she protested, digging for candles in the press beside the range. As they finished eating, Sean told tales of dining in Ghana, of carrying a single candle into the kitchen to check on the meal, leaving his company to carry on chatting in the dark.

At the meal's end, Sean showed them all a photograph. No elephant this time, rather a young woman, smiling, whose fine teeth Nora would have known for a Yank's anywhere. And if father and son were still somewhat hesitant, by bedtime the breach between them was no less mended for that.

Later, hearing a step on the stairs, Nora lit a candle and rose from the bed. Waiting in the hall, she met Sean coming back up. "Do you not know we've the facilities within now?" she softly admonished.

"I'm in Africa yet," Sean whispered. "Even where there's a toilet, you always go out to save on water."

"A great shortage of water in Ireland," Tom laughed as Nora got back into bed. "He's lucky he didn't drown out there." As he reached to extinguish the candle, Nora caught a tell-tale flash of blue.

"Don't tell me you found it?"

"In the brack you had hidden in the scullery," Tom teased.

"I'd have thought treacle bread was treat enough," retorted Nora. "So tell me, where did you find it?"

"At the bottom of the wardrobe at bedtime. Maybe it was in the cuff of my good trousers since the funeral, and fell out this evening?"

"It was my prayers to St Anthony," Nora said. "Patron of lost things."

"Aye, that too," Tom assented, blowing out the candle. Lying there, they listened to the rain overhead—until it became for Nora tiny dreamlike fruit, falling onto a tin roof beside a tranquil sapphire sea.

TRANSPLANTS

First published as a short story, 'Transplants' evolved into a novel, *Nighthawk Alley*, from New Island Books in 1997.

I KNEW Fintan was a piece of work the day I hired him. "There's no bowling team?" he jokes as I hand him a pair of coveralls off a nail in the garage. Maybe it was a case of one spider knows another—both of us Irish? Only compared to Fintan, I'm definitely more the garden variety kind. "No team unless you start one," I tell him. "Meantime you start at seven tomorrow."

He shows up at seven too, which itself is unusual for Irish. Not that anybody, Italian or Portuguese, is much better these days. The Greek kid I fired was always late, but Evangelis was probably on Chinese time anyhow, crazy about karate. It so happens the coloured guy Fintan had me hire shows up on time, but Lionel comes later in the story.

It's slow that first morning, even at the pumps, and by noon I lose sight of Fintan. Just when I'm figuring him for a half-day wonder, I spy him in a corner of the lot, picking up trash from the overgrown grass. Now I garden myself at home, but that patch of weeds and dog shit is so hopeless I don't even police it. "Any money is mine," I say when he finishes, only to hear him ask have I a grass hook?

He was the same way about the rest room as I shortly discover. "What are you using on the toilet bowl?" I inquire, barely recognizing it. "Coca-Cola," he tells me. "I'll buy some Ajax," I say, "so you won't be out of pocket." "Not to worry, Mickey," he says. "I was buying them out of the till."

Mention of the till makes me worry, but I get some Ajax anyhow, and pretty soon Fintan has the place so you can eat off the floor. Which leads to our first tug-of-war. "If I leave it unlocked," I explain, "every bum off the street'll be in there."

"Bums need a toilet too, Mickey," he laughs. "And if it's clean, they keep it so."

The door stays locked, but Fintan opens it for any derelict, most of whom, I admit, admire its tidiness. "I could clean my razor in the urinal," one guy marvels, making me wonder if I'm running a garage or a hotel?

Our location in Central Square, five blocks down from City Hospital, and midway between O'Brien's and The Shamrock Inn, ensures a certain class of foot traffic at all hours. Winos, junkies, and loony tunes, we get them all. Meanwhile Maggie and I still live the other side of Mass Ave, down in Cambridgeport, and I still walk to work each morning. The Square has run down of late, which usually means the developers can't be far behind, only this time I think they've gone bust, too. Anyhow, the Port is still lovely in spring: the odd magnolia in bloom, forsythia coming on, tiny maple seedlings where the sidewalk has cracked. There are even elms yet along Western Ave, great lofty trees under which these three tall, skinny, coloured guys sit in lawn chairs each morning early. "Rice farmers from Haiti," Fintan informs me when I remark on them. "One of them now runs the numbers for the Haitians," he says, however he knows this stuff.

Fintan himself is about ten years in America. From Donegal, he worked a few years in a garage there before emigrating. I left Dublin myself around that age, though at nearly sixty I must have thirty years on him? There weren't many cars in places like Donegal when I departed Ireland, but it happens Fintan is an ace mechanic, even troubleshoots the electronic stuff in the newer models which I don't touch. "People nowadays are driving appliances," I tell Fintan. "Toasters, not cars."

It's nice having another Irish around, somebody who understands just how different the States are. "You could live on what's thrown out over here," Fintan says, and he's right, of course. Forty years here and I'm still amazed at what people discard. Trash day is the best, with seventy-dollar shoes or freshly ironed trousers in rubbish bins at the kerb. Fintan has fairly furnished his rented room that way, and I ask him to look out for storm windows for the small greenhouse I'm building at home.

"What drives me mad," he says another day, "is how people here insist on happiness?"

"Have a nice day!" I jeer, but he has the bit in his mouth by now.

"'Happiness is only the premature profit on imminent pain,'" he quotes some Irish poet, whatever that fellow was sniffing.

"You should garden," I tell him, but Fintan says he coped enough spuds growing up in Donegal to last a lifetime.

Anyhow, he's good with customers as well as cars, especially like I said, the non-paying kind. A couple of older dipsos en route to the City Hospital detox floor now occasionally stop by to sing 'Danny Boy' or 'Kevin Barry' for us. "St Mary's is two blocks down," I tell him, "you want to lead a choir." Fintan tells me his mother used to write 'Do you ever miss Mass, son?' "Truth is," he laughs, "I don't miss it a bit!"

Word travels of course, and soon we're a port of call for any number of tramp steamers. Before long Fintan has names for most: the Philosopher is this skinny alkie who's always staring into space, while Mario Andretti has a wheelchair he moves by shuffling his feet along the road. My favourite is Father Flanagan with the stubble and dirty collar who pretends to be collecting for some charity. Fintan gives him a buck and the next day he's back, mumbling the same pitch. "Father, I gave yesterday!" Fintan laughs. "Oh yes, thanks very much, God Bless," the padre mutters, moving off.

"They're like stray cats," I tell him. "Feed 'em, and twenty-four hours later they're back."

"Cats eat too," responds Fintan. Yet it beats television all to hell, like the afternoon this floozy and her boyfriend stagger past the garage, thumbing a lift. Amazingly a car stops, only to have your woman pass out spread-eagled on the hood, her pal doing a drunken stumble dance beside her. The driver blows his horn, then shouts out the window, "If you want a ride, get off the fucking hood!" Another time Mario Andretti overturns his wheelchair out front. "Hold on," Fintan stops Lionel from going to his rescue. "He'll get attention now," Fintan says, "plus money." Sure enough, a couple of pedestrians give him both.

I wouldn't wonder Fintan takes an occasional dollar from the till for a hand-out, but I don't bother much with Mass anymore, so I figure it's only what I'd be putting in the collection basket. I draw the line, however, at leaving our loaner unlocked in case one of his Apostles needs a place to kip at night. It seems in Donegal they often found somebody asleep in their loaner, who couldn't quite make it home from the pub. "At least they *had* homes to go to," I point out to Fintan.

As it is, we do an occasional tune-up for this guy with some kind of muscular ailment who actually lives in his 1969 Plymouth. The car is a rat's nest of tins, newspapers and blankets, and reeks of piss besides. I can't get near it, but it doesn't take a feather out of Fintan. "I don't have an address," the guy says when Fintan goes to write up a bill. "How about Plymouth Inn?" Fintan cracks, causing Lionel to just shake his head.

Lionel, as I said, got hired thanks to Fintan. A few coloured have always come in, but not many, which I'll admit, suited me just fine. Most usually show up first thing mornings, after cruising all night. They don't get out during a tune-up either, just sit in the car sharing a beer or a joint. Anyhow, one week Fintan mentions this coloured mechanic he knows, and how hiring him would be good for business. It happens we're short-handed, Evangelis having left for a career in kung fu, but I couldn't see hiring a coloured. Or 'black' as Fintan, who'd teach his grandmother to suck eggs, keeps informing me. He keeps at me too, until I finally agree to take the fellow on part-time. Lionel looks like an aging middleweight, shaved head and all, but it turns out he's good under the hood, and honest far as I can gauge. What's more, we begin to pump some gas for those neighbourhood brothers who drive to work instead of cruising Mass Ave all night.

To be honest, Lionel is easier to figure than Fintan, who I sometimes think has some furniture missing. "Imagine being a pond skater," he says one morning. "Surface tension, not gravity, would rule your life!"

"What's a pond skater when it's at home?" I inquire, struggling with the rusted water pump on a '77 Nova.

"A bug that walks on water," Fintan hands me the proper wrench. Later that afternoon I'm admiring this classy MG pulled up at the pumps. "Nice as it is," Fintan tells me, "it's hardly a substitute for coming to know yourself."

"Piss off!" I reply, in case he's taking the mickey out of me. In fact it's hard to draw a bead on him at all. Some days he's in foul humour, a real anti-Christ, the next morning all sunshine, dispensing alms to the poor. I doubt he sleeps much, judging from the yarns about the whores and hustlers in the Hayes Bickford on Boylston Street, where he often sits up half the night drinking coffee. Sometimes I get the feeling he's perpetually ahead of himself, leaning against the garage on a slow afternoon like he were waiting to become a mechanic again.

July comes, and if there's a smell of ripe garbage in the alleys, at least there's sun in summer, unlike bloody Ireland. The sumac trees throw their saw-toothed shadows, and at home the cat crouches on a chair by the kitchen window, waiting for a breeze. One morning at the garage I arrive to find all hell has broken loose. "Mrs Kelly is waiting for you," Fintan warns me as I pass the pumps. "She finally caught on?" I ask, spying her husband Paddy slumped in the passenger seat of their Ford.

"Aye, she caught on all right," Fintan laughs.

I don't know how long we'd run that scam, all in aid of providing her poor husband with a little beer money. "Charge her for a quart of oil whenever we fill up," Paddy had requested, "and I'll collect the money off you inside?"

"You son of a bitch," Mrs Kelly shouts at me in the office. "Charging me two dollars every week," her face flushed, "for an empty can of oil?" I hadn't the heart to tell her different, though it cost me a steady customer. Afterwards Fintan tells of an uncle in Donegal who ate only brown eggs. It proved no bother to his aunt, until the day his uncle found her boiling a white egg in a pan of tea.

"Marriage is like a military campaign," I explain.

"You and Maggie aren't so bad," Fintan says.

"When you're gardening, you're not fighting."

"You can't garden in winter?"

"So I do a few chores Saturdays. Sundays I go down the basement where I've an easy chair and have a couple of drinks. When the wife comes home from Mass, I bang on the pipes with a hammer once or twice so she thinks I'm working. When I come up for the dinner, she looks at me and says, 'You've had a couple?' 'I had a couple,' I tell her. 'Just enough to keep the rust off.'"

Fintan had a girl friend when he started at the garage, but I gather she gave up on him. A nice girl from Mayo, she came by once for a fill-up. "She said I was a high-maintenance boyfriend," Fintan tells me with a puzzled laugh. I noticed Maggie took to him quick when he came over for a Sunday dinner, but that's kind of her way, given we never managed to have any kids. Yet there's something about Fintan that makes women want to do for him, because Mrs Lynch his landlady is the same, wanting to fix him bag lunches and such. What they miss, I think, is Fintan's at heart a man's man—as most of us are. Which is not to say he was particularly crude or anything. "I couldn't get fucked with a fistful of fifties," I heard him tell Lionel after he started drinking on the job, but that was the booze, not Fintan, talking.

It began then in August to go wrong for him. Fintan always kept a bottle in the back room for any Apostle in a bad way, but now he begins to hit it himself. "You're going to end up in O'Brien's," I warn him, "watching Candlepins for Cash."

"Just enough to keep the rust off," he replies. Later, two kids come by looking for used spark plugs—to make hash pipes, would you believe? "Fuck off," Fintan tells them, which is—while not bad advice—not his usual style. I notice the toilet isn't so clean anymore either.

Even days now when he's cheery, there's an edge to it—as if his engine were racing or something. "They're going to bury you in that Caddy," he tells this customer so fat he can hardly walk, and both Lionel and I hold our breath till the guy decides to laugh. Something is clearly out of whack, but people, unlike cars, don't have timing belts you can adjust, or little red lights like a washing machine, indicating an overload.

One afternoon pumping gas, I hear this bellowing in the garage bay. Inside I find Mario Andretti seven feet up on the lift, cursing a blue streak, while Fintan pokes a grease gun underneath his wheelchair. "Get him the Christ down," I yell, "before he falls and breaks his goddamn neck."

"Not to worry, Mickey," Fintan says, "I locked his wheels before I took him up."

"You're pushing it," I reply, as Fintan hits the air handle which lowers Mario, wheelchair and all. Mario is shook up, whatever about the bottle in his lap, his tongue moving back and forth like a windshield wiper.

"No drinking and driving," Fintan admonishes as Mario wheels off, but it doesn't strike anybody as funny. Watering my tomatoes that night, however, I decide a stunt like that at least differs from indifference. Which is more like what most of us feel for the Marios out there.

A month later Fintan disappears. It's early October, and a few bums sit mornings in the laundromat on Prospect Street, soaking up the heat from the dryers. One Monday I arrive to find a note from Fintan in the till, saying he'll be back in a few weeks. There's also some forty dollars missing, but I owe him that much easy for overtime; besides, money is definitely not what Fintan's about.

That afternoon Lionel tells me of some credit card scam Fintan was on to. It seems you pay this party in the billing office fifty bucks, who then tears up your charge slip. "Fintan was going to fly to Bermuda that way," Lionel explains. I say nothing, though I doubt Fintan owns any plastic to begin with.

Over the next weeks I wonder if he'll be there as I walk to work. There's a real sting in the air now, too sharp for the Haitians who have deserted their elms. I puzzle that displacement—from rice fields to city streets is even more of a stretch than from Dublin or Donegal to here. Transplanting is tricky, which is maybe why I was always trying to get Fintan to garden. As if by putting in a few vegetables, he might also put down a few roots? Whenever I pull weeds at home, I hear my father cursing the slugs in our tiny Dublin garden.

Lionel still believes Fintan's basking on a Bermuda beach, but I worry he's more likely sleeping rough over a hot-air vent. Not many Apostles call in anymore, though Mario Andretti drove by yesterday on metal rims, the tyres gone off his wheelchair. He looked even grubbier than usual, unshaven with a threaded lump on his brow. From what Fintan told me, Mario lives in a plywood box between two tenements down in Riverside, however he manages in the dead of winter. It's a funny thing, but I'm now actually noticing the derelicts throughout Central Square, like these two winos slumped yesterday against Libby's Liquors on Mass Ave, as if beached by a receding tide. I'm also seeing the other transplants I've taken for granted over forty years, stopping today to stare at three Chinese on a bench by Magazine Street, the eldest cutting the others' hair.

The other funny thing is Lionel and me. He's full-time now, and working me hard to take on his cousin too. Of course Fintan had a cock-eyed theory here, also. "There's a nod you give in Donegal," he explained, "just a wee twist of the head to whoever you meet. I've done it for years here, Mickey, and blacks are the only ones who ever read it."

"Soul brothers," I mock, but Fintan insisted there was something to it. "Secret signals, Mickey. One spider knows another."

Anyhow, Lionel and I sometimes have a beer after work in this bar on River Street, where there's maybe one or two other white guys besides myself. It's there I finally learn about the bowling team thing.

"Fintan was living someplace like Arizona," Lionel says, the coloured barlights reflecting off his shaved head. "He had a job with this huge diesel outfit, lived in an apartment complex with a pool and closetful of clothes."

"How'd he mess that up?" I ask. "Boozing?"

"Hell no," Lionel laughs. "Crazy dude thought it *was* messed up!"

"I don't follow," I say.

"Fintan said the whole set-up just freaked him out. So one day he pushes his car off a cliff, throws his clothes after it, plus a brand-new bowling ball."

"Puzzle me that?" I say.

"Go figure," says Lionel.

Walking home through the slush on Pearl Street, I wonder might Fintan return come spring? At heart, however, I know he was more a once-off annual than a perennial, poking its head up every year. Or, better yet, a "garden escape"—like the fuchsia, first planted at Irish big houses, that now grows wild everywhere.